ALAN SHIVERS

Europea Halls 2: A Summer in Budapest

First edition

This book was professionally typeset on Reedsy.
Find out more at reedsy.com

I want to dedicate this novel to Uncle Gerry and Aunt Det. You both know why. I love you.

Acknowledgement

How do I even start this one? So much has happened since the release of "Europea Halls" and I am incredibly grateful to everyone that has shown support over the past months.

To my graphic designer: thank you for once again creating a gorgeous cover. It fits in really well with the first novel and I am excited to see what you'll come up with for book three.

My lovely proofreader Jenna, you sure have a lot of patience correcting my punctuation. I appreciate your feedback and your constructive criticism helps me grow more than you realise.

I feel incredibly lucky to be in contact with the beautiful Aroace community and I have learned a lot from my sensitivity readers. I hope I have done the aromantic asexual community justice. Isapun, Jasmin, Astrid, Moonlit and so many others: you know who you are, thank you.

Another group of people that have shown really strong support: my ARC team.

Without your early reviews and feedback I would certainly struggle getting the word out for my novels. Thank you to everyone for taking the time to read my book, comment, post videos, reviews and so on, it means so much to me. A special thanks to Stephanie, Sharron, Pebbles: the three of you have gone way beyond and promoted my book to so many people. I'm eternally grateful, honestly.

My fellow slasher authors, I feel like such a lucky bunny to have met so many lovely souls over the past months. A special shout out to Sarah Jules and Emerald O'Brien. I appreciate and respect you both. Oh, and to whoever is reading this: read these authors' books - thank me later.

A big thank you to the podcasters who have gotten in touch with me for interviews as well, I am (slowly) learning how to get over the initial awkwardness of being on film thanks to your generosity and kindness.

My friends and family: so many of you have reached out and bought copies of my debut and spread the word to others. My parents are still my biggest support system in life - and yes, they still hate horror, but luckily they love me.

To all my buddies from Brussels (my current home), Budapest, Manchester (my previous homes) and beyond: thank you for being such great friends, I love you all to bits.

Blanche, my sweet dog, you might never understand this, but thanks for being the best assistant out there. Your snoring is soothing me as I'm writing this sentence.

And last but certainly not least: a massive thank you to everyone who has picked up a copy of "Europea Halls 2: A Summer in Budapest". The fact that you are following these protagonists on their journey past my debut is really exciting! I hope you enjoy the summer slasher.

Much love,
  Alan

TRIGGER WARNING

As this is a slasher novel, there are many scenes full of violence, blood, and gore and descriptions of deceased people. The book gets quite tense, which might be too intense for sensitive readers.

Other topics touched upon are trauma and PTSD. Viewer discretion is advised.

Chapter 1

MARIJA

"No way, that's them!"

"Who?"

"Those massacre survivors—you know, we talked about them just the other day!"

I can tell by the blank expression on his gorgeously simpleton face, Christian has absolutely no idea what I'm on about. I roll my eyes. "The Europea Hall survivors from last year. They were in the news all the time."

There it is, yup, slowly but surely; he finally gets it.

"For real? What are they doing here?"

I shrug my shoulders. "I'm not sure, but my guess is they probably need a break from Brussels after all that has happened to them."

One of the four glares at me in distrust. Guess I won't be making friends here anytime soon. I can tell by Christian's expression he is up to no good. He's smirking. Ah, I hate it when he does that. "Chris? What?"

"I'm going to go talk to them."

I yank his left harm. "No, you will not. Are you mad?"

"We both know that's a rhetorical question, love. Just a little chat."

Before I can say anything, he walks towards their table at the bar. I shift behind him awkwardly, holding onto the door frames as the train seems to be picking up speed.

"Christian, wait! Maybe they just want to be left alone. I know I would—"

Too late. Cockiness has won over kindness, again. He is such a pain to travel with at times. There's still a long trip ahead of us; the night train to Vienna takes thirteen hours, forty-seven minutes (I'm a girl who likes her details—don't judge). If he ends up chatting to random people all night, I will lock myself up in our private carriage. Social battery running on empty, alert. Close friend or not, I need my time alone. As Christian heads towards the four semi-famous teens, it hits me how jammed the bar carriage is. Everyone is up for a party tonight, apparently. There are only about seven tables, but they're all crammed with people our age and one older couple who won't last too long in this room, by the looks of it. The two good-looking bartenders are obviously overworked and underpaid, as the beads on their foreheads are glistening in the sun, which is beaming through the carriage windows. This is quite a nice night train though. The ones I've taken in the past were not nearly as clean and crisp as this one. The Dutch and Belgian flag pattern is everywhere just in case no one knew who funded all of this. It's a new era for train travel in Europe, and I'm glad it is picking up popularity-wise.

"Hey, guys! Heading to Vienna for the festival too?"

They all look up, quite confused. *Read the room man, come on.* I am two seconds away from bolting to my room for the night when the guy in the group replies, "No, we're on our way to

Budapest, actually. But there's no direct night train, so we'll catch a ferry from Vienna in the morning."

"Oh right, Budapest. Cool city man, you'll love it!" Christian leans over, full of confidence, shakes his hand, and gives him a kiss. "My name's Christian, nice to meet you!"

"Karel," the guy replies with a hint of a smile on his face. He seems kind. Attractive as well. I'm a sucker for long hair on guys, definitely when it's tied up in a messy man bun like that. Jawline for days too —swoon.

"This is my girlfriend, Ingvild." She reaches out a hand to Christian, which is quite odd, as people our age in Brussels usually greet by kissing each other on the cheek. A handshake without a kiss means distance. The name Ingvild sounds Scandinavian though, so maybe they're not big on the Belgian kisses. Who knows?

One of the other girls speaks up now too. "My name is Karla, and this is my better half, Oliwia." To my surprise, they both stand up and give Christian a kiss.

"She means other half, not better." Oliwia winks at Karla and gives her a coy peck on the cheek. They're so cute together: couple goals.

He looks back and signals me to come over. The group follows his gaze. Ah, crap. I have a gloriously gory book waiting for me in the bunk bed. But no, now I need to socialise with mass murder survivors. What do I even say to them? Congratulations on being alive?

"Her name is Marija." Thanks Chris, I am perfectly capable of introducing myself. I muster up the courage for a round of chitchat and put on a wide smile.

"Hey everyone, lovely to meet you all!" Somehow my smile appears to soften the atmosphere in the room. I walk over to give Ingvild a kiss, but the rocky train tracks catapult me right into her arms. Smooth, Marija, real smooth. That's one way to greet someone.

Ingvild cracks up. "You are going all in with the hello, I see. Very American of you, a hug and everything!" She pats me on the back and winks at me. I take a moment to compose myself and have a proper look at the group. How are they all so stunning? Ingvild's eyes hit a bright ray of late evening sunlight as the emerald green proudly fills the room. She's a stunner, just like the rest of them. I can tell they come from money, just looking at their fashion styles, but I guess that shouldn't come as a shock, seeing as they go to Europea. They've all changed from the photos I saw on the news though. Like, a lot. Karel's hair is definitely way longer, and I don't think he had a stubble before. Ingvild looks like a bohemian plant connoisseur, with her flowy dress on and wavy blonde hair up to her waist. She definitely had bangs before. Karla has bleach blonde hair now, cut up to her shoulders. I couldn't keep up with that style—too much purple shampoo time for me. I'll stick to my light brown. Oliwia is definitely the one who stands out in the group. She has pink, almost neon-like middle-length hair and dark heavy makeup. I wouldn't want to mess with her, but maybe that's just prejudice. My dad's a biker, and he's the nicest guy you'll ever meet, bar none. Funny, though, how they all have different styles, but they do somehow come across as a coherent unit. I look so average compared to them—so does Christian actually. I can't wait to be in Vienna and see the rest of our friend group, 'cause he is already doing my head in. He's alright in small portions, definitely one-on-one, but in groups like this, he is just so damn loud.

Ingvild nudges me. "So, you two are on your way to the

4

electro festival, I assume?"

"Yes, we are. We've been going for the past three years. The rest of our group flew over, but we wanted to take the night train."

"Way nicer, right? No hassle with customs or check-in."

"Exactly! Plus, I don't want to fly for such a short distance. Shame the trains are so pricey though."

The silence is a bit uneasy. Dumb comment. These people don't have to be careful with their money. I tug on my washed-out hoodie and look down at the floor.

"I get you," Karla replies. Thanks for saving me. "They should really lower their prices on night trains."

Another silence. Christian gives me a sympathetic glance and continues: "So why Budapest?"

Ingvild and Oliwia exchange hastened looks. Oliwia takes the lead. "Ingvild and I have been meaning to go for ages, so this year we decided it was time to go."

"I can imagine you all need a getaway," Christian interjects. My heart sinks. Things were going so almost-well. Way to put a damper on the chitchat show.

Karla straightens her back. "What do you mean?"

"Well, with the murders and all. We've seen you in the news. So sorry about what happened to your friends."

"I see." They all look at each other, a wave of sadness filling the carriage, the weight too heavy to bear. The people around us are catching on and the silence cuts through the entire carriage, anxiously waiting for release.

"Look, Christian, I appreciate the talk; but if you don't mind, we'd like to hang out, just the four of us for a bit. Would that be okay?" Karla's politeness makes it even tougher to watch.

"Come on, Chris, let's go. Thanks so much, everyone, for

being kind to us. We didn't want to intrude on your privacy. Have a lovely trip." I run out of pleasantries, so I grab Chris's elbow and push him out of the bar. No more beer for him.

I turn around once more as we walk off, and Ingvild gives me a little wave.

"I knew you would do this! They were being so nice to us, and you mention the murders. Don't you have any tact?"

"Another rhetorical question!" He laughs, but I don't. I am so embarrassed about the entire situation I could sink into the ground and find myself a cozy little bunker down there to spend the rest of my days.

"I'm sorry, I'm sorry. I know you hate it when I do that."

"Then why did you? You couldn't have just left those poor people alone?"

"They are a lot of things, but they're not poor. You know those Eurobrats— always feeling better than the rest of Brussels."

"You know what I mean. Anyway, let's just go to bed, we'll need all the sleep we can get before Electrica starts."

He looks baffled. "Already? It's like ten!"

We both hear the party going on in the carriage next to us, the music getting more intense by the minute. Some obnoxiously drunk tourists (probably Australian, 'cause they're singing *Wonderwall,* and one of them is playing a ukulele) are running across the corridor, dressed up in some sort of cultish hoods. Stag party probably. Christian's eyes light up.

"That sounds fun! Sure you don't want to say hi to them, Mari?"

I snort. "Quite sure, thanks. Feel free to hang out with them. Honestly, think I'll just listen to some music and read a book if that's okay with you."

6

He is definitely annoyed. I do feel a bit bad, but I know I need to recharge before plunging into four days of boozing with a group of eleven people.

"Fine. as you wish, melady. I might go say hi to those guys out in the corridor."

"Have fun!"

"You too." Ah man, don't give me that look. Like a rained out little puppy.

"I'm sorry, Chris, I know you want to party, but I need a bit of time to myself before we meet the rest. Don't take it personally, please."

"Okay, I get it. Well—" He slaps his hands on his lap. "I'm off then, enjoy your book. What are you reading, by the way?"

"*You're Not Supposed to Die Tonight.* That slasher by Kalynn Bayron."

"Oh right, the one you mentioned in class. Sounds cool, actually."

"You can read it when I'm done." I know all too well he won't read a single page of my book, but I realise I've been a bit mean to him.

"Sure!"

I jump up. I'm a bit sweaty. What time is it? I must've conked out right after Christian left. It's pitch black out, and the only light coming in is some sepia tinted streetlights flashing by. I check my phone. I've been out for over an hour. Looks like we're almost in Germany. I glance outside again and take in the moment. The feeling of freedom rushes over me, wrapping me up like a cuddly blanket. This is exactly what I've been missing in my life: travel. Those exams really took it out of me. Can't wait to drop chemistry next year.

My mind flashes back to the bar. There was something over-whelmingly heart-crushing being around those four people. The things they've been through, the people they've lost. You could tell they all truly tried to be open and welcoming, but the sadness in their eyes was unmistakable. How could you trust anyone after all of that?

My phone pings. I'm a bit rattled and spaced out, but that sound always brings me right back.

Unknown Number: *You're supposed to die tonight.*

Chapter 2

CHRISTIAN

The Aussie, or one of them—not sure how many there are in the carriage—hugs me tightly. His BO is kind of making me want to vom, but that might be the beer. Just one more, just a teeny little sip and I'll go back to Marija. I just wish she'd cut me some slack sometimes. She's always on my case, as if I'm such a horrible human being to be around. The Aussie burps right into my face. Grand. The mix of cheap beer, weed and something garlicky hits me in all the wrong places. Wonderful elixir.

Time has really flown by. These guys are super welcoming. Nice change from those four before. What a funeral vibe they gave off, damn. The fact that the Oliwia girl looked like a goth chick on crack didn't help either. Not talking to that motley crew anymore for the rest of the trip, that's for sure.

The guys around me are chanting along to *Teenage Dirtbag*. Not too convinced about their taste in music, but I'll stay a bit longer. Maybe one more shot, actually.

"Dude, could you pass me that vodka bottle?"

Aussie flings the bottle at me, and for some miraculous reason, my reflexes are still intact. The train conductor has passed by our carriage twice to ask us to keep it down, but that won't happen with this crowd. There's nine of them, and they came to have a good time. They've thought of everything as well: speakers, booze, snacks, costumes—they are all dressed up in some weird gothic-looking hoods 'cause it's their graduation party trip.

Aussie squeals with joy as some generic noughties rock tune comes on. "This is my jam, man, my jam!" They all start dancing in a circle, so I join in. Everyone is holding onto each other's shoulders like a Greek sirtaki on speed, spinning around a little bit too—

Oh no.

I fling open the carriage door and jolt towards the lavatory at the end of the corridor. Occupied, you've got to be kidding me. I've got exactly zero seconds left before I spew my soul out. I sprint towards the other side of the corridor. Luckily, the light next to the lock is green. I click on the "Open" button, but it's one of those toilet doors that open painfully slow. I wait for it to open, rocking back and forth trying to keep it in, until I can finally enter. There it is, all at once and everywhere. I'm trying to aim, but no use in aiming when the force is this strong. I feel bad for whoever has to clean this up.

My knees are weak, and I've got the cold sweats. Great start to a holiday. I'm *so* not telling Marija about this.

I place the palms of my hand on the cold sink in front of me to gather my thoughts and strength. I don't have much of either right now if I'm being honest. I look at myself in the mirror in front of me and exhale. That feels a bit better. It's only now that I realise I haven't closed the toilet door. It's still wide open. Let's hope most people are deep asleep by now, or they would've enjoyed my melodic symphony from their rooms. I hastily click on the close button, so I can have a moment to recompose myself.

My phone vibrates. Probably Marija wondering where I am.

Unknown Number: *I hope you enjoyed your last beers.*

What is that supposed to mean? Is Marija pissed off at me still?

A figure in a dark hood with his head bent down steps in front of the door, blocking it from closing. I shriek and lose my balance for a second.

"Aussie? Dude, you scared me! Can I have a moment?"

The figure lifts his head. A horrifically petrifying mask gazes right at me.

"Is it you, man? What is up with the mask?" I try to stay cool, but the gnawing sense of dread is making it harder than I'd like to admit.

Then it clicks. I've seen this mask before. It's been on the news. The killer from Brussels, it's the same mask. My gut tenses up; I need to get the hell out of here, now.

I try to push the hooded shape in front of me, but he is strong, way stronger than I am. He cusps my neck with his right hand and pushes me deeper into the toilet, locking it behind him. I frantically attempt to claw my way out of his death grip and scream for help, but there's nowhere to go. The door is shut tight. My screams are being drowned out by the music played a couple of rooms down the hall. The grip around my neck is becoming stronger, making it harder to breathe.

"What do you want? What is your problem?" My voice comes out squeaky and raspy. I need to save my breath before I run out of air. How can I get out of here? The groin. I knee the figure in front of me in the groin, and he instantly loosens his grip. I flop down onto the toilet floor. It worked, the shape is confused and bends over in pain. Be quick, think, how can you— the mirror. I smash my elbow into the bathroom mirror and take a shard to protect myself. I turn around and smash the "Open" button, waiting for the door to react. I can see a part of the dimly lit corridor; escape is near.

Then it hits me, a protruding pain in my upper back. I've been stabbed by a shard from the mirror. My left arm jolts up erratically as the figure pushes the piece of mirror deeper into my body. My entire nervous system is on high alert, and I start twitching, which makes me drop the only protection I have. A scream comes tumbling out from deep within me as the glass scratches my flesh and bones.

I fall down and the spasms continue. I try to focus and stand back up, but the shape behind me pushes me back down with his foot, stabbing me once again with another shard. I taste thick syrupy blood in my mouth, far too much blood. The toilet door is now completely open. I can only hope for someone to come out of the wagons and help me. But I'm alone. Just him and me. I can't see very well anymore; it's all becoming a bit blurry. A telling feeling inside my stomach signals me to prepare for the worst.

She's there. She's here.

"Mari, help!"

Chapter 3

MARIJA

It takes me a moment to register what I am seeing in front of me. At first, I thought Christian had fallen down 'cause of the beer fest inside his body, and the figure behind him was trying to help him out. Then the crimson red hits my irises. That mask, those four survivors. The message on my phone, the looming sense of danger. It all clicks.

"Mari, help!" He reaches out his hand to me whilst being pushed down by the person behind him. I run towards him—there's no way I'm leaving my friend behind when he needs me the most. As I approach the pair, the hooded figure grabs Christian's locks and lifts his head. Chris's eyes are full of despair and angst, slashing deep into me. Those are the eyes of someone who knows they are about to die. I know it, and he knows it.

"Chris!" I yell out, not sure why. The figure pulls out what looks like a piece of glass from Chris's back and pierces his neck from behind, the sharp tool cutting all the way through his neck, the sound too horrific to even describe. His eyes turn the deepest pool of black as the blood spews out rhythmically until there is no more beat to his heartbeat.

I stand there, motionless. A morbid painting splotched out in front of me. The mask now looks straight at me. I scream as loud as I can and make a run for it. I move towards the first door I can see and knock on it, but I notice he is right behind me, so I keep running and knock on each passing carriage door, hoping for someone to come out and help me. Nobody. The absence of help only makes me want to fight more.

"Somebody, please help me! I'm being attacked! Someone wants to kill me!" I can barely believe the words as I utter them. I find it hard to focus, overwhelmed by shock and fear. *Keep moving, don't slow down.* My knuckles are hurting from the incessant beating, and the tears are climbing to the surface. I need to find a way out, a way to safety. Where do I go?

As I sense the killer's breath down my neck, I snap out of my thoughts and sprint on further along the corridor, past yet another carriage. He's fast, I'm not sure how long I can outrun him. That thought triggers a moment of panic in me. A shallow breath escapes me, as I continue on what appears to be an endless path. How is nobody helping me? *Cowards.*

I run past the third carriage, loud party music overpowering my screams and tears. He is getting closer to me. I'm not giving up—I need to throw him off somehow. In the midst of my sprint, I make a quick U-turn, facing the killer. *You've got this.* I tighten my fists and run towards him. My chest is tight, sharp pains hitting my neck. He seems taken aback for a second. I push him into one of the corridor windows and continue my path in the opposite direction. The moment I pass him, however, he pulls out a large butcher's knife and stabs my left arm. I nudge him with my right elbow, more out of anger than anything else. I bite down the pain and continue forth, even more determined to make it out. Somehow, I can barely feel the throbbing discomfort.

I am confident this is not it; I won't allow it to be. I plot my way along the train, carriage past carriage. Each metre, he inches closer behind me. I'm becoming a bit wobbly and light-headed. A moment of doubt fills me as I stand in front of one of the exit doors. Before I can gather my thoughts, the killer smashes the emergency exit button, which swiftly opens the doors. The sharp wind from outside mercilessly hits my body. I'm not sure whether I should jump out and hope for the best or push him out. Second option, definitely. I try to push him out, but he is far too massive to even slightly budge. I wrestle with his almost immobile body, which resembles a heavy statue made of solid stone. He grabs my head and smacks me down to the floor, extending my left arm, which I notice now is bleeding heavily.

"What are you doing, you freak? Let go of me!" The confidence leaves my body the moment the killer pushes my left hand outside. What is his plan? He yanks my arm further down until— *oh no, there's no way.* My stomach churns as I know what this means.

My hand violently hits the soil next to the train tracks. It all goes so fast. I can't see for a split second, the torment too intense to cope with. I hear this metallic sound of my bones being pulverised. I'm too afraid to look, but I need to see it. My hand is gone. Fleshy strings of dark orange unnaturally flapping in the air, accompanied by the gushing blood flying off into the night sky. This time I do feel it, the overwhelming realisation of powerlessness. As the wind howls mockingly through my entire being, the darkness of the night engulfs me. I close my eyes and try to find peace. Pointless. There's no peace to be had here.

The figure pulls my head outside and knocks it down with one of his boots in one brusque move. The entire world slows down for a moment. I see myself partying with the other eleven, dancing away to electronic music in Vienna. Smiling, golden hour setting on my bronzed skin. Hugs from the group, our flowy tops and colours against the city's backdrop. A small moment of happiness flourishes in my soul.

The gravel next to the train tracks is tauntingly approaching my vision. I hope I won't feel this anymore. I hope the knock onto the ground makes me unconscious before I die. The gravel on the ground looms in until it's too late to escape.

Chapter 4

OLIWIA

The gentle swooshing sound of the train tracks soothes my mind. The others are deep in discussion, but somehow I lost myself halfway through when the topic turned to European policies. The lanterns outside brighten up our sleep carriage every other second. The rhythm of its dance reminds me of the pendulum swinging back and forth in hypnotherapy.

Vera is her name. It took a lot for me to reach out to her. I had tried all of it, the whole shebang: my local GP, psychotherapy, Cognitive Behavioural Therapy, acupuncture. You name it. I started out quite traditionally, but the deeper I started hurting, the more I opened up my mind to alternative routes. As proud of a person as I might be, there came a point when my body caught up with the trauma I'd largely been ignoring.

At first I had the occasional spasms before sleep, nothing too frightening. Then the numbness came, it was usually the left side of my body. I would think back to, well—you know—and my body would quite literally go numb. I didn't comprehend what the hell was happening to me. I thought I had coped with it. Naive, sure, but it's not like I had any prior experience to how to get over your friends being—.

Phase three was the balance issues. I would fall down on

the street in the middle of a walk, without any warning or anything. That part was frightening. I didn't know how to trust my own body anymore. Then what I later learned was called dissociation came into play. It'd feel like I was walking left or right next to my body, not feeling the impact of my own gravity.

Then the panic attacks hit. The first time I thought I was having an actual heart attack, it was the most intense pain and fear I had ever experienced. Well, maybe. I've gone through some things, haven't I? Anyhow, once those became more frequent, I felt more and more isolated. I tried not to show it, but Karla and Ingvild could see right through me. It wasn't until Ingvild put a copy of *The Body Keeps the Score* in my locker that I accepted something more than just fear was weighing me down. The first time I allowed myself to cry—and I mean full-on sob fest—was when my first psychotherapist told me my disorder was called PTSD. Post-Traumatic Stress Disorder. I mean, everyone's heard of it, I'm sure, but I didn't think all these tiny things were part of it. Being terrified of any loud noises, your body being in constant fight or flight (and in my case, often freeze), the chronic pain all over my body, the blurry vision with the muted colours. Then there's the smells, the lights, anything that could even hint at a reminder of back then can be a trigger.

To be fair, the attacks are less frequent than they used to be. I still get them about once a week. It used to be daily, sometimes even multiples times a day. Those were the weeks I locked myself up in my bedroom. So there, I do see improvement. I know I've got a long way to go, but I'm getting there, wherever "there" is.

CHAPTER 4

So, back to Vera. I'm venting a bit here, I'm fully aware, but it's been one hell of a ride. What I like so much about hypnotherapy is that I never had to talk about what had happened. She just asked me what my aim was. She didn't focus on what was wrong, but rather what outcome I wanted for myself. It started small from an outside perspective (but for me these were massive steps): walking with a good balance again, not feeling numb any longer. Feeling like I was a part of my own body. Not forcing a smile but actually smiling. Not frequently, sure, but occasionally. She's a boss, that one; she doesn't really allow me to feel bad for myself. A little moment of wallowing—cue the violins—and then she tells me how it is. That I have a choice. As difficult as it may seem. Choose the right path, ownership, simple happiness. I repeat those mantras every single morning on my balcony. Sometimes I even smile. Corny or not, it helps me.

For the longest time I kept it all to myself. I didn't want to burden anyone with the symptoms. The moment I finally opened up, though, everyone else did too. I had become so wrapped up in my own little misery bubble that my empathy levels had plummeted as well. I didn't see how much pain Ingvild was in too, physically and mentally. Her medical rehabilitation was by far the toughest. I know I wasn't there for her enough when she needed me, I don't think I had the capacity to. Not at that time. It's a good thing she's got Karel. He's been there every single step of the way. But still, it should've been me. It took a massive falling out for her and me to get close again. For her, the survivor's guilt had taken over most of her life. I think she still finds it difficult to be around me sometimes. I guess we all grieve in different ways.

The pink hair colour was perhaps a cliché move, but a very

19

conscious one at that. I needed to shake things up, but I didn't really have the guts to go for a full-on makeover until Karla and Ingvild told me they'd join in. Fair enough, I wouldn't call their new hairdos as dramatically different as mine, but they went for it as well in their own way.

Karla is definitely into my new look, a lot. Can't complain on the sexual front. Looking at her now, as she is neck deep in the discussion, my heart melts. It does every single day, honestly. I love it when she's in one of her deep talk modes. She can talk anyone else under the table; they don't stand a chance when she's got a point to make. She notices the way I'm staring at her.

"What is up with you?"

I smile. "Nothing, boo. I was listening."

"No, you weren't. You couldn't care less about politics."

Karel and Ingvild both laugh. Karel teasingly replies, "Let's switch to the Marvel universe."

"Hey, come on now. You make it sound as if I only talk about Marvel."

Karel makes a "Well, don't you?" face and I give him a (kind, I swear) slap on his elbow.

"I know about other things too! Ask me anything about Surrealist or Cubist painters, for example."

Ingvild locks eyes with me and nods. Budapest and the Surrealist gallery. It reminds me of our talk underneath the weeping willow at Europea. I'm glad we are here, on our way to Budapest. Not with the two of us like planned, but on one heck of a double date. Ingvild takes my hand and squeezes it. She doesn't have to vocalise it; I know she is thinking the same.

I know about other things too, thank you very much, Karel. Or rather: I used to. I have not mentioned slasher films or the horror genre in general since then to the others. It's a part of myself that I have locked away firmly, and Pandora's box ain't got nothing on my Slasher box. It's this weird thing—anything that used to excite me terrifies me nowadays. Roller coasters, horror films, crowded places. I've become a bit of a party pooper, but I'm working on it. I'm working on a lot. PTSD is an absolute bitch, I swear.

I jump up from my bunk bed. The hairs on my neck stand up within a split second. "Did you guys hear that?"

Ingvild's eyes show me she heard it too. "What was that?"

"Screaming, I think?" My heart protests fiercely in my chest.

"Let me check." Ingvild stands up.

I pull her back instantly. "Ing, stay here!"

Karla and Karel exchange quick looks, I'm sure they think I'm being dramatic. Ingvild gets it though. Karel stands up instead of Ing.

"I will just open the door for a second. You girls stay here."

Karla rolls her eyes at his "heroic" move. He is a nice guy, but he has these moments where he believes we all need his help. We do need help—that's a fact—but so does he. He has definitely become more on edge as well. It's odd how those things work. Karel and I are definitely the jittery ones, whereas Ingvild and Karla have only become stronger. Or that's the way it seems to me anyway.

He shuffles around a bit and walks towards the door handle.

"Be careful," I whisper.

Open it already. Are you being dramatic on purpose?

He opens the door. I hold my breath. No more screams. He peeks his head out. *Great, dumbass, that's how you get decapitated.*

21

"So? Anyone?" Ingvild asks with a meek voice.

He turns back to us. "Nobody, I think anyway. It's all black out there in the corridor. Can't see much."

My curiosity takes over, so I stand next to him and peek out as well. He holds onto my arm. This time I'm not too annoyed at him for being "the man.", I'm petrified.

Nothing. Just a pitch black corridor with some faint lights at the back where the toilets are.

As I close the door behind me, I feel someone walking past us.

Chapter 5

INGVILD

"I swear someone passed by the moment I closed the door!"

"I believe you, Livvy," Karla replies, "but it could've been anyone. I mean, we are on a sleeper train."

She's rather offended. She opens the door again; no one. "Don't you think I know that? It just didn't feel right."

She still stands next to Karel, who is holding onto her arm for dear life.

Karla pulls her down towards her and gives her a tight hug. Karel positions himself next to me as well.

"It doesn't feel right, Karla. That wasn't a normal scream!" Karla strokes her back and slides her head into Oliwia's neck.

"I know, baby, but there are a lot of people partying out there. We've been hearing screams all night."

"This one's different. Why would someone pass by the moment I closed the door?"

"Because there are hundreds of people on this train, Livvy. We are all together, in our own carriage. You are safe with us." That clicks.

Oliwia's body gradually melts deep into Karla's arms.

Why can't I do that? That used to be me. I was the one comforting her, but something inside of me blocks me from doing so.

At first I thought it would've brought us closer together. We've lost our friends, all of them, except for each other. But having her around me, seeing how frequently she freaks out or jumps up at the slightest sound, exhausts me. There's no denying my love for her. I care deeply; I always have. But I need to take care of myself too. Whilst she was going through her grief, I was in the hospital, one physio session at a time. Becoming stronger physically, sure, but I didn't even allow myself the time to think about my emotions. I still have the occasional flare-ups of inflammation and excruciating pain, most specifically when I am stressed out.

We won't go back to how it was before—I'm not naive. Not anymore. But perhaps there's a stronger, fresher tie we can create out of all the misery of the past year and a half. I'm convinced there's a way out of this limbo, I just don't know how or when yet.

Karel holds my left hand and kisses my temple. He knows me so well by now, it kind of scares me. I don't even have to tell him when I need a moment or when I feel angry. He just lets me be myself, without judging.

Oliwia's body tenses up again. What now? *Stay calm, Ing, you know she's hurting.*

"I told you all going on a trip was a bad idea! We're isolated from our families and the guards. And that message—"

"No," I reply firmly. Oliwia glares at me open-mouthed, ruffled by my answer to her non-question.

"We need this trip. I am the first to admit that I walk around with guilt every single day for being alive. But I do know we

24

deserve this. We've been through too much to just punish ourselves on the daily and stay in Brussels. The city and the boarding school will be there when we come back. I just need a breather. Those places hurt."

Liv tenders up her eyes. "Those places?"

"The halls, our dorm rooms, the Marolles, mont des arts, Grand Place. All of it; there's too much history." The others remain silent.

"You must know what I mean, Liv. You still haven't gone back to your movie club in Ixelles."

"I-I wouldn't know what to do or say there," she admits in a defeated tone.

"So you get me. Five days, don't you think we owe this to ourselves? All four of us? It's not like we have run-of-the-mill relationships or friendships here. We need a bit of lightness. It's all been too heavy."

"You're right. It's just that message I received in January. I still feel like there was more to it."

Karla takes over. "More to it than a prank text? The police have traced it back to that douche Erik. He was just bored with his own life, trying to scare us. He knew about the wording of 'team' because I had stupidly spoken up about it in that local interview."

"The police, boo, really? They were of no help whatsoever when-"

I don't want to hear the rest of that sentence, so I cut her off. "Alright, alright. We get it. That message was seriously messed up. But Erik apologised, didn't he? He's a loser who wanted some attention. It's been over six months. Nothing has happened since."

Karel chimes in. "Exactly, we're safe, like Karla said. I agree with Ingvild."

I hold in a small giggle. Why am I such a child whenever he's around?

"We need to look out for each other, girls. We've all gone through hell and back. Let's just live it up in Budapest. Oh, that reminds me!" He pulls out his phone and draws up Google Maps for all of us. "Look, I have saved a couple of those ruin bars and spas in my wish list. Did you all read that article I sent you?"

We reply with a dramatically slow "yes" in unison, teasing him and his planning skills. There's a cool breeze entering the room and the conversation. Smart move, Karel—I have to give it to him. He's one of the most emphatic guys I've ever met. Not every guy would be okay travelling around with three girls. Karla jokingly said once that he's one of the girls, and he wasn't even offended. I wish all guys could be like him. But you just need one good one, according to my mom, who texts me at least twice a day since that night. She was the one I needed to convince the most about leaving Europea Halls and the guards behind for five days. She's more scared than I am. She's come through; in all fairness, she has. We've grown way closer than we used to be. I did not see the move coming. Both of my parents living back in Brussels. The ripple effect of a little trauma—it's got its perks too, apparently. That reminds me: I should probably text her.

I unlock my mobile, and just as I go to start texting my mom, I receive a message.

My palms are instantly sweaty. Unknown Number.

No way. My stitched-up hand releases a pang of sharp heat. Stress pains, not now. Don't show the rest, stay calm. I breathe in, count to five through my nose, and exhale through my mouth. Count to seven, or—how many seconds am I supposed to do that breathing technique thing again? I open the message. This is it.

Welcome to Germany. Your service provider is Orange. The same rates of calls and texts apply.

Chapter 6

KARLA

Oh, it's my turn? Alright, well, insert an Austrian accent as you read this, everyone. My name's Karla and I'm Oliwia's girlfriend. What, they know that already? I'm new to this, give me a moment.

I'm the only one who's still awake, as per usual. Livvy is lying next to me—I'm the big spoon tonight—comforting her as much as I can. Ingvild's not big on PDA, so she decided to use the top bunk and let Karel lie down on the bottom one next to us. No idea how her snoring doesn't wake the rest of them up, but then I guess the swooshing sounds of the train tracks overpower miss's rattling. It's not exactly a luxurious train, but it'll do for the night. The mattresses are basically glorified cardboard, and the promised "freebies" ended up being apples and on-board travel magazines promoting Amsterdam, Brussels, and Vienna. But maybe I've gotten a little too used to luxury over the years. At least this is adventurous. It's just us, not our families taking us on some high-end trip, but the four of us, discovering a new city on our own terms. Ingvild turns over, and the entire bunk starts frantically shaking. Karel is in too deep of a dream state to even notice. Let's hope the beds—and us with it—make it through the ride.

Tonight was actually pretty nice. Oliwia's moment of tension was completely understandable, and I know she and Ing have some things they need to work out, but I truly enjoyed our political debate earlier on. That's when I lose Livvy though, but you can't share all of the same interests, right? That'd be like dating myself, and believe you me, one of me is more than enough. I can usually pretty much talk anyone under the table, but Karel stood his ground. I'll give it to him. Maybe I should ease up on the tough love this trip. He's been nothing but kind and understanding to Ingvild.

A dark grey flash hurries past the window. For a moment I think I see a hooded man's reflection outside, but I let my rational brain take the lead. Pushing away the fear isn't the way to go, according to Oliwia, but it works for me. I think. I exhale slower than I usually would. My neck muscles are stiff, but that might be because of these cheap bunk beds.

Looking at the other three, I am grateful. We've all been through a lot. Granted, Oliwia and Ingvild have lost more than Karel and me, but still. It's not like I haven't killed anyone. I often think about Lucija and LeBeaux, that entire showdown on the gardens of Europea Halls. I try not to show my girl too much, but the nights are the worst. When she finally falls asleep, I'm the one staring into the gaping night. I want to sleep, but I know what awaits me there. Awful nightmares, and always the same ones. I'm the one who ends up decapitated, not the detective. The moment the ax slices through my neck, I wake up.

Every. Single. Night.

29

I was close to telling Livvy once, but she'd had such a bad day after hypnotherapy that I couldn't bring myself to open up to her. She doesn't need to know *everything*. I don't think she'd even know what to do to help. And therein lies the problem. The only problem. Genuinely, I adore my girl and I respect her resilience and proactivity, but I do wish our relationship could be a tad more balanced. I've become the caregiver and it makes complete sense, but at times I wouldn't mind someone doing the same for me. No Karla, that's a shitty thing to say. It's not her fault she's not there yet. She will be, soon.

Ingvild's snoring intensifies, I had no clue that was even possible. I crack a smile, which was needed. I know we all feel it, this weight. But it's been too much to cope with, really. It's high time to shake things up, live a little. I need museums, cafes, spas, and ruin bars, pronto. In the morning we'll arrive in good ol' Austria, my native home, and I can't wait to speak German for a hot second before boarding the ferry to Budapest.

Push that feeling away. There's no one looking at you from outside.

They're dead.

Chapter 7

KAREL

This bathroom is way too tiny and wobbly to have a proper shower in, but I did the best I could. Some rays of early morning sunshine are proudly shining through the minuscule window. It compensates for the lack of pressure on the shower head. Today is a new day. We're in Austria.

I decide to literally let my hair down for once. The man bun works wonders on my jawline—Ingvild's words, not mine—but today is officially day one of our trip, and I want things to *feel* different, so I make the conscious decision to *look* a little different too. We should arrive in Vienna in about twenty minutes, so time to dry up.

It's nice to have a moment to myself. I might need it now and then in case the vibe gets too suffocating, but I'm rather sure it won't. Actually, I was surprised how nice Karla was to me when I woke up this morning. I know she has a soft side to her, but it's not the easiest one to spot. When we all first started hanging out, I felt like I was going to get cancelled every day, 'cause in all fairness, I did say some right-out stupid stuff. I had never had a lesbian couple in my friend group before. So let's just say I learned quickly how old fashioned some of my preconceived thoughts were. When I said cis straight white guys have the toughest time these days jokingly, I could tell Karla started opening up to me. Educate rather than cancel, she always says. I like that about her. That woman needs to become the president of something—whatever—soon. Her rhetoric trumps mine even though it kills me to admit it. I took BBC Public Speaking training courses because I wanted to become a more confident public speaker, but for her, it just comes naturally.

There: all dried up. My hair is looking fine today, if I may say so. Definitely not a man bun day. I hear the train announcer's jolly voice: "We will shortly be arriving in Vienna Hauptbahnhof."

I cannot wait to take the girls to all these cool ruin bars. Such a unique concept, too, turning old soviet structures like hospitals into quirky arty (hopefully not too farty) bars. I'm ready for this, Brussels can have its crap and trauma; I'm here for a good time. I walk out of the bathroom and into the hallway. The sun is really going for it today. Great start, we needed this.

As I walk past the corridor, I notice what looks like some drops of blood right in front of the toilet. I swallow—it hurts a bit—and nervously scan the corridor. Nothing out of place here, right? Sleeper trains are not exactly renowned for their high-end toilet hygiene. Someone must've gotten into a small drunken brawl. That's all there is to it.

Right?

Chapter 8

KARLA

We've definitely brought too much luggage for a week's trip. All of us are dragging along our suitcases with the sun forcefully hitting down on us. The breeze helps though. It's not exactly healthy seaside air, but the wide Danube River heartily welcomes us as we stumble towards the massive ferry. I thought I'd hear more German—Österreichisch, to be more specific—and feel some sort of nostalgic heimat vibe, but I mostly hear Dutch and English around me. I haven't been back home in Austria for years now.

My family and I first moved to Brussels when I was about eight years old. We used to live in Innsbruck, and even though I do still miss the dramatic landscape of towering mountains and crystal lakes, I had grown accustomed to Brussels' flashy lifestyle fairly quickly. There is quite a large German-speaking community in Brussels, and a small part in the east of Belgium actually speaks German as their first language, so I never felt too out of place. Belgium being trilingual also helps with shopping. Everything has to be written in French, Dutch, and German, so I always feel at home when I am reading the ingredients in the supermarket in my mother tongue. Still, I'm Austrian at heart. There's no nature like that in Belgium;

there's not even any mountains in the entire country—just some hills and forests.

I hear a girl's scream in the distance. My breathing shallows. *Stay cool, Karla, it doesn't need to mean anything.* I peer back and notice the Prater, the permanent fun fair in Vienna looming from the other side of the city. Those screams used to be a clear sign of fun and letting loose, but something about hearing a bunch of girls screaming on fun fair rides now makes my skin crawl. We all have our triggers.

At least I was able to order four drinks in German. I'll take what I can get. I ordered four Radlers, as I don't want to get us all too drunk before we've even arrived in Budapest. The ferry ride takes about four hours, passing by Bratislava in Slovakia first. That's plenty of time to get seasick, or how do you call it when you are on a river cruise—river sick? The ferry itself is a bit of an iron extension to our night train. It all sounds rather fancy, going on a river cruise, when in fact, this ferry looks like it could fall apart at any given second. It's large and heavy on the concrete, sure, but it's definitely past its glory days. It seems to agree with me as the creaking of the flanks intensifies.

As I hold onto the cheap plastic cups (come on now, these could've easily been paper) filled with our low alcohol Radlers, I step outside onto the main platform as the wind hits my hair. It's like a rush of relief and excitement at the same time. It did make me spill a tiny bit of the drinks, as I did not expect that much of a shock to the system, but I genuinely don't care. This feels great, finally. A smile fills my entire being as I notice the atmosphere on deck. All these young people talking, drinking, taking photos of the Danube; and in the middle of it all, my

34

friends. I don't think I've seen them look this happy in months. Actually, in over a year. As I step towards them, Livvy notices me and beams with joy.

"What did you bring us, boo?"

"Four Radlers. I thought it would be a good idea to pace ourselves."

Karel pulls a grimace. "Those things are nasty and full of chemicals."

My heart drops, I hoped I chose well. He instantly notices. "And I love it. Great choice!" He apologetically winks at me, grabs his drink, and gives me a hug. I guess we're still fine-tuning our communication styles, the two of us. We're getting there though. I've been trying to be kinder to him, and he is lighter and jollier, without a doubt.

Ingvild raises her cup and shouts, far louder than her usual self: "Let's cheers, everyone, to a great trip, to us, to a new adventure, and to moving forward! Cheers!"

We all erupt in cheers and smiles, a moment I want to hang onto. I grab my phone from my left pocket and take a selfie with all of us, including our drinks obvs, in it. I've never been one to take many pictures, but I want to document this trip. It feels monumental in the best of ways.

"Do you want me to take a photo of you four?" A gorgeous brunette with hazel eyes asks. I stumble over my words a bit and try not to let it show to Oliwia how taken aback I am by her beauty.

"Me? Yes, that's, sure, fine!" The eloquence has taken over, I see. How I managed to pull Oliwia, I have no idea.

The brunette takes our photo and once she does, I notice she is accompanied by two other equally beautiful people: one girl

35

with long ash-blonde hair and blue eyes and a guy with olive-coloured eyes and a buzz cut. The girls are both curvaceous in the absolute best way possible, while the guy is as jacked as they come. His t-shirt is a couple of sizes too small, but I have a feeling that was rather a conscious decision on his part. Even I can tell his pecks are well-defined and prominent.

"My name's Agueda," the brunette tells us and gives us all a peck. Oliwia and Ingvild seem hesitant to talk to them, but I'm not letting them dampen the mood.

"Karla, and this is my girlfriend Oliwia, and my friends Ingvild and Karel."

Everyone greets each other, and as the kisses are floating around the windy deck, I can sense my friends loosening up a bit. Good, I don't want a repeat of the sleeper train debacle. I learn that the blonde is called Andreea and the guy's name is Mihails. They are all smiles and enthusiasm, and I am absolutely here for it.

Chapter 9

OLIWIA

Karla is definitely eyeing up that Agueda girl, but I can hardly blame her. I mean, she's sexy. We have talked about flirting with other people in the past, and we are both fine with it, as long as we're transparent and honest with each other. We did decide on monogamy, but we're both open to a threesome if the situation would ever present itself. Karla's eyes are most certainly gleaming with the thought of that prospect as we speak. I perk up a little as I notice I'm not actually jealous. I'm glad I'm not that petty. We've gone through too much to let someone pretty come between us. Even with—well—curves like that. *Focus, Oliwia.* I decide to turn to the guy named Mihails, who funnily enough Ingvild is unsuccessfully avoiding looking at. Karel is standing up a bit straighter, poor guy.

"Mihails, you said? Cool name, where's that from?"

"Latvia. I'm from Jelgava."

"Sorry, where? I mean, I know Latvia obviously, but that city? I've only been to Riga."

"That's fine." He smiles. Those dimples though, I can understand why Ingvild is blushing. How did this ferry just randomly throw three hotties onto us?

"So, did you fly into Vienna or?"

"No, we started our trip in Brussels and then took the night train here."

That sets off a small alarm bell. "Oh, right. So did we. Funny we didn't see each other on the train."

"Well, it was quite packed, wasn't it?"

I suppose he's right. "It was. Sorry, I got sidetracked there. You were telling me about Jelgava?"

"Well, most people haven't heard of my city, it's about forty kilometres away from Riga."

"I see, cool. And how about the rest of you? Are the three of you all friends, or have you met each other on the ferry? What's the situation?" I actually surprise myself. I don't think I've felt this interested in other people's stories in a long time. It's refreshing not to wallow in my own grief for a change.

"The situation?" He chuckles again. "Agueda and Andreea met each other on an exchange programme."

"Erasmus?"

"Exactly, that's the one. They both studied in Manchester together four years ago." That must mean they are in their mid-twenties. Do they even realise how young we are? Never mind; I'm not telling them unless they ask.

"Oh, cool. And what's their connection with—?"

"Me? I met both of them about two years ago when they had a reunion in Riga. We clicked on a night out and have been travelling together ever since. We're a good squad, the three of us."

"That's sick! So you just hit it off, and now you're exploring Central Europe? Are you getting off at Bratislava, or are you all going to Budapest as well?"

"Budapest. Can't believe I still haven't been."

"Right, me neither. The city where east meets west."

I'm just babbling away here, but I don't think he minds one bit. The conversation is flowing naturally. He nods at Karel, trying to include him.

"So what is the plan in Budapest?"

Karel pulls a smile, but I'm not too sure how authentic it is. I still don't get how he isn't more self-confident. Half of Europea is always drooling over Karel and his nonchalant looks. But then again maybe this here is the appeal: he doesn't understand how attractive he actually is. I mean, I'm full on gay, and I can see it. Why wouldn't I?

Karel clears his throat. "Well, I have saved some spots on my map."

"Such as?" Mihails' gentle tone is finally diffusing the tension.

"The obvious ones, like the ruin bars and the spas."

"That's a given. We should go there together!" He hastily scans all of our faces, as we are all focusing on him and Karel now.

"I mean, unless the four of you don't want to, I don't mean to impose." The first hint of uncertainty hits his face.

"We'd love to, right girls?" Karel asks us. We all agree. There's a lot of nodding, enthusiastic giddy smiles, and planning happening right now. Mihails and Andreea take a look at Karel's Google Maps as they go through the planning, whilst Agueda and the rest of us all get to know each other. It's a bit of a chaotic mess, all of us cackling and asking each other a million questions. It's a pace of life I'm not used to anymore, and I can tell my brain is trying to keep up. A sliver of PTSD pokes at me as I feel the brain fog coming in, but I pull a Karla and consciously push it away. Not now—I'm enjoying myself.

I blink a couple of times to zoom back into focus and exchange numbers with the group.

And then there were seven.

Chapter 10

KAREL

Damn, this guy's muscular. Out of all the people on the ferry, he had to be the one we end up talking to. Ingvild is trying so hard not to look at him too obviously, which makes it all the more obvious. Whatever, I'm the one she has chosen, so I shouldn't be like this. *Get a grip, dude, come on.*

The seven of us have been talking and drinking—Karla's plan flew right out the door—for some hours now, and they are really a fun bunch to hang out with. It's highly welcomed, this new carefree vibe. It makes us all a little more chill too. Even Oliwia is in a talkative mood, it's good to see that side of her come out again. She always used to be the one talking to random people at parties, so good for her, reclaiming that part of her character. We have decided to meet up tomorrow night, to explore Instant together. It's the most famous ruin bar in the city, on the Pest side of town. Apparently, it's like a labyrinth of different dance rooms and art installations. Can't wait. We should arrive in Budapest in about half an hour, and the four of us decided it'd be best to explore a bit on our own first and take our time to get to know the city. Plenty of time to hang out with these new people tomorrow.

Mihails continues his questioning. "So, are you also staying in a hostel on the Pest side? We're in the seventh district."

"Oh right, the old Jewish quarter? Good choice! Apparently that's where all the nightlife is at. No, we're staying in a hostel on the Buda side."

That's a blatant lie. Budapest is split up into two, the posher hilly Buda side with its castles and mansions, and on the other side of the Danube there's the flat Pest side, where the Parliament and the nightlife scene is located. I don't want to tell him we're staying in the Hilton. That'll only make us sound like snobs. I could've done with a hostel experience, but I'm not sure the others would've been up for that.

He frowns a bit. "A hostel on the Buda side? Okay, I thought they were mostly on the Pest side."

"Right. Right, they are, but we found a nice little hostel on one of the hills overlooking Pest. It's close to the Chain Bridge."

Another lie. Well, partly. We are close to the bridge, but that's about it.

"I suppose you'll just have to make your way over to the fun side tomorrow night then." He pokes me with his elbow. I lose my balance for a second but try not to show it. This dude is strong. I straighten my back for the umpteenth time and nod. "Will do, man."

In the middle of our talk, this sense of dread creeps in. A set of eyes appears to be burning into my neck. I flip around and skim the platform, but no one in particular is looking at me. This is the second time I've felt this though. It's almost as if we've brought something or someone with us from Brussels. I gander at Oliwia, but she seems to be fine in the crowd. I know it's not her thing anymore, but somehow it's *me* who tenses up thinking about how many people there are on this ferry and how many opportunities there are for a killer to hide here.

"Charles, you okay man?"

I cough. "Karel, my name's Karel."

"Sorry about that, like I said, I've never heard that name before."

"No worries, dude! You weren't far off either. It's the Flemish variation to Charles." I stare at my feet for a split second, trying to recompose myself. "I'm fine. I was just wondering if we are getting close."

Mihails takes his phone out and checks the time. "We should be there soon. Yeah, about twenty minutes, I'd say."

"Thanks for checking." A silence grows between us. It's an awkward one at that, as we don't know each other yet. We both join in with the girls' conversation, as they are still on full social mode.

Andreea senses that we are listening in to them, so she directs her next sentence at all of us. "So we'll see you tomorrow at nine for pre-drinks at that square? What's the name again, Mihails?"

"Déak Ferenc Ter."

"That's the one. I won't be able to remember any of these Hungarian names, I can tell you that already. Déak something something."

Ingvild happily replies, "Sounds like a great plan!"

As we are approaching Budapest, we give a kiss to our three new holiday buddies and walk down the cabins to claim our luggage.

There's that feeling again though; why can't I shake it off? Is someone here, waiting for us?

Chapter 11

INGVILD

I can tell Karel is tense straight away. I'm not sure if it's because of Mihails or something else, but he always thinks he can hide it so well. I have learned how to read the signals. That erratic look in his eyes, his stiff shoulders. It makes me feel guilty, as I am usually the one venting to him, but I forget he's gone through stuff too.

"What's up, Karel? You're tense."

"Am I?" He is taken aback.

"It's fine, whatever it is. You can tell me."

Oliwia and Karla are walking a bit behind us, rolling our luggage onto the docks in Budapest.

He leans in and whispers to me. "I had this sense of urgency, like someone was watching me."

I can't help but look behind me quickly, but I don't see anyone. The girls notice my glare and wave at me.

"I don't think anyone's here that we should be afraid of, hon. Do you need to sit down for a moment?" I hold his hand. It's burning with sweat.

"I'm fine. It's fine. Really."

"You don't have to hide things from me. We said we'd be open to each other."

He softly exhales. "I do feel tense, but I know if I walk it off, I'll be fine. Let's just continue towards our hotel, and we can relax a bit there."

"Okay, but be honest with me, even if we're on a trip and we're here to have a good time. Don't omit things from me just to make me feel safe. I'm here for you too."

I squeeze his hand. His shoulders drop a bit.

"Thanks, Ing. You're the best." He kisses me on the lips and pinches my chin.

People had told me about the grandeur of the city, but I'm still in awe at the first sights of Budapest. We walk next to the imposing Chain Bridge, with its gigantic lions and deep grey iron swirly tubes. I read it was blown up during the Second World War but then got reconstructed right after the war ended, connecting Buda and Pest. There are plenty of other bridges now too, but this one stands out. It's a beautiful mastodon of a construction. Ahead of me I can see the lush green hills of Buda, with the neo-baroque castle in the middle and a higher, sharper looking hill on the left that carries a statue of a woman holding what looks like a flame on top. I thought the Communist statues were all removed after the Berlin wall had come down in '89, but this one still remains proudly, looking over and guarding the city. On the right of the castle, I see a group of cute sandstone turrets and towers. Oh right, that must be the Fisherman's Bastion, the one that Disney got inspired by. We'll have a lot to visit here. Each landmark looks as monumental as the next, and that's just on one side of the capital. I'm sure I'll get my Art Nouveau fix too though. —It won't all be brutalism and neo-styles. The Art Nouveau—or Szecesszió, as it's called here (yes, I also did some research, thank you very much,

Karel)—buildings here are far more bombastic and tall than in Brussels, where it's mostly small town houses full of details. Here, the roofs stand out. I can already see some emerald green and mustard yellow tiles on top of some villas in the distance. It instantly makes me excited about travelling. Facades galore. I have never been to Hungary, so I love the idea of every single street being full of new impressions. I've missed this.

Oliwia points at the Hilton Hotel, up high. "It's all the way up there? Do we really have to walk with our luggage?"

"We could take a quick Uber," Karla suggests. Oh no, girl, you should know better. Oliwia and I have been avoiding any kind of Ubers or taxis since what happened to Ayat. I notice Oliwia's jaws clenching. I don't want her to feel tense again. This trip I want to do better for Liv. For all of us.

"Let's take a bus. I'm sure it'll go to the top of the hill. Karel?"
"Yes?"

"Could you look up the best connection to go to our hotel from here?" I lower my head slightly, speaking with my eyes. He gets it.

"Right, of course—straight away."

Liv smiles at me. "That was kind of you, Ing, I appreciate it."

We step out of the bus and walk in front of the entrance of the Hilton. All four of us are used to some pretty luxurious hotels, but this one is something else. There are four tall marble columns at the main entrance, supporting the neo-classicist roof. The columns are carved out with awe-inspiring intricate details. From a distance it looks as though they are swirling towards the heavens with their diagonal Corinthian foliage. Oh yes, the geek in me—or old soul, I know mom—is properly waking up now. I let out a little squeal. Oliwia cracks up. "Will this quaint little abode suffice for you, boo?"

"You know I love myself some architecture."

The others light up as they see my enthusiasm sparkle. This is promising to be one heck of a trip: we've already met three new people and we'll be sleeping in absolute beauty. Let's hope the rooms are just as nice.

Yup, they are. Oliwia's father made sure we got the two largest private suites. The hotel receptionist gawked at Oliwia's passport. All of us get the occasional jealous glances when they see our diplomatic passports, but hers tops ours. No idea how it never made it into the news that Oliwia is aristocratic. We used to tease her by calling her Countess Oliwia, but it made her feel very uncomfortable, so we stopped. I don't even think the teachers at Europea know. I'm sure the head mistress does, 'cause she's getting more than a pocketful of sponsoring through Liv's parents. In any case, on moments like these I'm glad to be friends with blue blood, the suite—en-suite, actually— is breathtaking. Karel and I have a direct view onto St Stephen's Basilica, the Chain bridge, and practically all of Pest. The opulent ceiling in our bedroom is decorated with leaf gold depictions of Greek mythology. There are meticulously hand-painted tiles with Hungarian folkloric symbols and elements throughout the bathroom and the deep green bathtub/Jacuzzi looks like it was imported straight from a Turkish spa. My favourite part is the balcony though. It stretches along the entire length of our bedroom and has four lovely teak loungers on it. The fresh flowers and potted plants add an extra homey touch to the otherwise stately rooms. Oh, I could live here. Well, maybe there's a bit too much eclecticism happening around me, but I can hardly complain, can I?

As Karel and I step onto the balcony, Liv and Karla wave from the balcony next to ours.

"Approved by the expert?" Karla semi-yells as the wind is picking up from the fifth floor of the hotel.

"Absolutely. You've done well, Liv!"

We all take a moment to appreciate the scenery around us. We've made it to Budapest. The strong gusts of wind exorcise the last remaining droplets of anxiety from my system. We're fine. We're safe here.

Chapter 12

AGUEDA

I'm definitely not in Portugal anymore. This city has an entirely different vibe to it. Andreea, Mihails, and I have been walking around the Pest side for the past two hours or so, taking it all in. The massive Parliament, Freedom Square (don't you even dare ask me the name in Hungarian), the basilica. So much to see here. Everything is so imposing and wide. All these big boulevards too. We don't have them like that back in Porto. The Jewish District, number seven, reminds me of the old Jewish quarter in Krakow. But again, bigger and bolder. Can't wait to explore these ruin bars. That Karel guy hyped it up so much; let's see if it lives up to expectations. District seven has gone through some serious gentrification lately, like any hip parts of European cities, I guess.

There's that man again. Shivers roll down my spine. I latch onto Andreea's arm.

"It's him. That creep."

"What, where?"

I point towards the end of the cobble street. "There, I'm sure it's him."

"How can you tell from so far away?" she questions me.

Mihails joins in with the disbelief. "Agueda, for real, you always think some guy is following you. The same thing happened in Barcelona."

That's offensive. It's not like I think the entire world revolves around me or anything. "Fine, don't believe me then. I'm telling you that's the same man I spotted on the ferry and the same exact guy who was staring me down in the Hummus Bar."

"Maybe he's into you," Mihails jokingly replies.

"Well, I'm not into him. Those eyes will haunt me in my sleep tonight. It really irks me that you two don't believe me. I'm not saying it to get attention, I swear!"

The two mellow down a bit. Andreea pets my shoulder. "Sorry, we shouldn't brush it off like that. What do you want to do? do you want us to go talk to him?"

He is still looking straight at me. How can the others not see how menacing he is?

"No, let's get out of here. Let's take some small side streets and go back to our hostel."

I'm relieved to be back in our hostel. Relieved and not relieved, 'cause I'm not sure whose idea it was to book a room with eight bunk beds. The entire space reeks of mold, perfumes, and toothpastes. The mix of it all makes me a bit queasy. But then, we couldn't afford anything more than this. Budapest has really gotten expensive over the past few years, plus it's high season. The couple next to my bunk are making out on the top bunk again. I'm not sure how much of the city they'll actually see, as they've been reinventing the meaning of tongue twisters since we first dropped off our luggage. I'm not doing this anymore once I turn thirty—no way.

The hostel itself is fine, not great, but it'll do. The building is basically a large slab of concrete divided up into several floors. One of those typical Soviet buildings from back then. It does have a cool edge to it, but the mural paintings are trying a bit too hard to be hip. At least there's a cute rooftop with a cocktail bar; I'm not saying no to that.

I wonder how Hungarians feel about all of these repurposed buildings anyway. I'm not sure how I'd feel with the past being so visible, yet it being inhabited by drunk tourists. That reminds me; it must almost be time for Happy Hour on the rooftop. I slip out my phone and unlock it. Oh right, it's been on airplane mode to save battery. I turn on the hostel's rather unsteady Wifi. Oh, five missed calls from my sister. Probably to talk about the baby again. And, yup, there it is. A dozen photos of the baby on Whatsapp. What's this one? An actual text message? Who still does that?

Unknown Number: *Can't wait to see you in Instant tomorrow night.*

How do they—? My mind works on overload for some seconds. My heartbeat makes it all the way up to my throat, where it picks up speed. I check the country code on Google. Oh right, it must be from one of those four people we met on the ferry, +32 means Belgium. They all live in Brussels. That's nice of them.

A flash of that creep rushes past my brain. No, it can't be him. How would that guy even know? It's those people from Brussels. It must be.

Chapter 13

ANDREEA

Agueda sits across the bed, scrolling through her phone with a focused look and furrowed brows. She's been adding some spots in the city to her list on Google Maps. I can see why she and Mihails get on so well. Those two do all the planning, so I can just tag along without even needing to feel guilty about it. I'm very much a spur-of-the-moment kind of person, so I throw in some off-the-beaten-path suggestions here and there. Together, the three of us work quite well.

In all honesty, I'm a bit relieved there's no tension between us anymore. Last time in Barcelona, Agueda admitted—not that she needed to be ashamed or anything—that she had previously hooked up with Mihails. I wasn't exactly shocked, but the timing was a bit off. She told me right after Mihails had kissed me in a bar. It all got fairly messy for a while, with both of us fawning over Mihails and him undoubtedly soaking up every moment of it. But there was no way I would end up being *that* girl, losing a friend over a crush, which is why I decided to— how can I put this? —I suppose, get over him. For the rest of the trip, Agueda and Mihails kissed a couple of times, which was not exactly the nicest of feelings after he had made out with me two days prior, but I explicitly told the two of them to go for it and that our kiss had only been a silly drunken mistake. Looking back now I most definitely downplayed my own emotions and confusion. I was hurt. I didn't know how to show or word it, but a part of my ego was bruised. It's not the best of feelings to be second option. However, swallowing my pride seemed like the only option back then. I did learn a valuable lesson in life: don't put aside your own emotions or pretend they're worth less than your friends'.

Agueda put in a proper effort to show she felt sorry by coming over to Cluj. She hadn't been to Romania before, meaning I got to do what I usually don't do too well: play tour guide. It came naturally that time, 'cause planning things to do around the city meant I didn't have to focus on how I actually felt.

We're good now though. I'd like to think we are.

Chapter 14

KARLA

I am thrilled yet confused by the menu in Napfényes Etterem. We ended up here for lunch because it is said to be the best vegetarian restaurant in town, so I got all excited; but now I am staring at the options, and there's too many yummy things to choose from. I am definitely trying the Goulash soup, we are in Hungary after all. Perhaps I'll just go with the mixed platter after that. If there's one thing I've learned after a day in Budapest, it's that their food is way better than Austrian food. Sorry, homeland, I love you to bits, but all these veggie options here—hard to beat. And there are Hummus Bars everywhere too. Plus, don't even get me started on their fresh lemonades; every bar seems to make the most original mixes. I had a raspberry basil mint (and three other ingredients I have forgotten about) lemonade at Mazel Tov yesterday evening when we went for dinner, and it's the best thing I've ever drunk. Yes, even better than Belgian beers.

We took it pretty slow yesterday evening. We had a nice little stroll around the Fisherman's Bastion and walked around the hills. Then we took a bus to go to Mazel Tov restaurant. Best Jewish cuisine ever. We didn't want to explore the seventh district too much yet 'cause we knew we'd go out there tonight, so we went straight back to the hotel and had an early night's sleep. We were half drunk, half sleep drunk, so it was much needed.

This morning we slept in—I think we all needed it. None of us have travelled since the entire spiel, so that sleeper train and ferry took it out of us more than we'd expected. Around eleven, we walked down past the Elisabeth bridge. Karel, our jolly tour guide, told us that it was named after empress Sisi from the Austrian-Hungarian Empire. I'm actually glad he's done his research, 'cause I love a good historical fact. I texted my grandma straight after, 'cause she always watches the Sisi films over Christmas. From there, we went to the covered market hall to buy some local produce like dried peppers, caviar (not for me, my veggie heart wouldn't cope), and smoked cheese. Okay, I'll admit it, we bought some small bottles of Palinka too, heavy stuff. I bought peach and grape Palinka, but even by just smelling them, I could tell I'd need food in my stomach first.

Which leads us back to now, in Napfényes. We all decide to share platters, so we can try as many different plates as possible, which was an excellent choice. Every single dish is beyond delicious. That's it; I'm moving here.

"I'm already sold on this city after one day," I mumble as I stuff more melted cheese in my mouth.

"Same! When I was doing all the research, I was afraid the city might be a bit overhyped, but seriously, what's not to love? Great food, brilliant views everywhere, this quirky mix of old rundown buildings with bombastic houses."

Ingvild chuckles. "You're turning into me."

"What do you mean?"

"I think I've infected you a bit with my love for architecture."

He smiles gleefully. "Well, that's not the worst thing to be infected by, is it?"

They're so frigging adorable together, I can't stand it. Almost like an old couple, but in a good way.

"I'm glad you think so." She turns red a bit. I swear, if I weren't in love myself, this much cheese in front of me would make me nauseous, but—oh right, there's more cheese. I take another big bite. I'll have to walk this off after.

Oliwia's been a bit quieter since we arrived at the restaurant. I want to give her the space to acclimatise, but I also don't want her to think I'm ignoring her being quiet. Ingvild and Karel act blissfully unaware, either that or they're overcompensating by being extra cheerful. I wish I could tell. There are always so many hidden emotions between the four of us; why can't we just put it all out there? What else do we have to lose?

"Hey, Livvy, what do you think of the food?" I enquire.

"Oh. Nice, yeah, it's really nice. All these different flavours and textures." That sounds a bit flat. I don't want to push her though. Ingvild looks sullen all of a sudden. So she *does* sense it as well.

"Tell us, Liv. We're here." There's something about her Norwegian directness that just works for Ingvild. It's not fake, it's not angry, but it's so straight to the point. I think that's why they're such good friends. Oliwia needs someone like that. I still struggle a bit to get the emotions out of her. Livvy's not even shocked, she knows her so well.

"Sorry. I don't want to be a Debbie Downer."

"No, you're fine. Just be real with us."

Karel chews on a tofu steak a little too carefully to be natural.

"I've had a bit of time to think. After we left Mihails, Agueda and Andreea, we were all on a high from meeting new people. But after waking up this morning, I realised I have trouble trusting them."

Karel swallows the tofu a little too loudly.

I kind of want to join in on the convo, but sometimes it's just best to let these two talk it out together, so I take some more cheese.

"I see. Well, to be honest, I think that's a very valid emotion to have. It'd be weird if we didn't have any sort of trust issues."

A tiny sliver of hope sets in Livvy's eyes. "So you feel it too?"

"Of course I do. I think we all do." Ingvild includes us, and both Karel and I nod. She's right. I want to embrace new people in my life, but it does feel a bit dangerous.

"I thought it was just me."

"This is exactly why we need to open up more to each other." I'm grateful Ingvild is saying the things I can't yet. "Otherwise we'll end up feeling isolated and misunderstood. I need time to trust new people too. But I want to."

"Me too, I promise! I don't know how though."

Karel chimes in. "Maybe don't over analyse the process this time around? Look at the trip as a learning experience on how to 'do life' again. That's how I see it at least." That man is smarter than I give him credit for at times.

"So I should let it go and go with the flow, you're saying?" Oliwia seems unsure.

"Yes, I know that's easier said than done, but give it a try this week. They can be your new trial friends. See how it feels for you to open up and meet new people, whether it drains you or gives you energy."

I realise we didn't have any of these types of conversations before the massacre. It was all about going out, school gossip, art, and language. Now we sound like a bunch of self-help gurus.

"Thanks Karel. I really appreciate that. A part of me couldn't fathom why three people who are obviously in their twenties would come up to us?"

Ingvild takes over again. "It's the pink."

"The pink?"

"Your hair, dummy. It attracts hipsters like moths to a flame." We all laugh. With that we all said what we needed to.

"Should we head back to the Hilton, chill out a bit there, and get ready for tonight? What time were we meeting them again, Karel?" I wonder.

"Nine for pre-drinks at that square with the ferris wheel. We could bring our Palinka bottles." That idea both terrifies and excites me. None of us are actually big drinkers. Oliwia and I go through months of sober phases, but this week I am open to being a bit more boozy than usual. As long as I don't lose control. Last time I was really drunk was when I drank my self-made punch at Czechia Night. The idea of being truly inebriated scares me because I don't want my senses to be blurred out. That's what happened that night. Tonight, I am going for tipsy with a hint of messy.

Chapter 15

INGVILD

It was so kind of Karel and Karla to go for a walk together to give Oliwia and I some space before going out. We are sitting on a bench next to the Freedom Statue on the sharp hill I noticed when we'd arrived here yesterday. The view is splendid; you can take in the entire city from here. There are quite a lot of tourists around us, but somehow I don't mind. The buzz engulfing us allows my brain to be mellowed out a bit. We sit here in silence, our knees touching. There's still so much to say, but is this the time and place? Is there such a thing?

The statue is holding up a palm leaf. I thought it was an olive branch at first, which would've made it even more symbolic to sit here. But still. This lady empowers me to speak up. I'm craving freedom too.

"I miss us, Liv." I expect her to be shocked, but she continues staring in front of her, teary eyed.

"So do I, Ing."

"But I still love you so much, you need to know that."

A tear rolls down her right cheek. She lets it roll. "I love you too, more than I will ever be able to express."

In the past these types of sentences would've cringed me out beyond belief, but now I know it needs to be said, because you never know when it's too late to say it. So I continue: "I wish I would've said that to them more frequently. Alzbeta, Ayat, and Marieke."

Now she does look up at me, rattled. We haven't said their names in—I'm not sure how many months. More tears flow down, from both our eyes this time.

"Those names. I am still so stuck in my PTSD. So many things trigger the attacks, and I'm scared to even say their names." She starts sobbing, first gently then more intensely by the second. We hold each other. She breathes in and continues: "Alzy, Ayat, and Momma." She cries even harder now. I can't control it either. "I miss them so much, Ing. I miss MIOLAA. Even if that bitch Lucija was part of the acronym."

"I miss them too. But listen—" I take hold of both her hands, wipe away her tears and continue, my voice shakier than I'd like: "We *cannot* give up on us. On ourselves and on each other. We survived it. We both have amazing partners, and we have each other. I don't want to carry all of this on my own anymore." Now I crack. I can't always be the strong one; I'm done with that. She holds *me* this time around.

"Neither do I. I need your old soul vibes in my life." Her eyes show me the kindness I've been missing for a long time. I haven't seen this side of her. It's just a glimmer, but it's there again. She speaks up: "I want to include them into our trip though somehow. Take them with us. They would've all loved it here."

"Absolutely. Ayat would've dived into the thrift stores in no time."

"And Alzy would've looked up some sort of Hungarian techno playlist for our pre-drinks."

"And Momma, well, she wouldn't have allowed Karel to plan

everything." Sorry Marieke, but we both know it's the truth. Liv and I smile. "They would've had to work together, but in the end, Marieke would've made up the entire schedule."

Oliwia agrees. "I have never met anyone as good at planning as Marieke."

"Me neither! Karel is a close second though."

"Don't tell him that. It'll break his heart," she jokes.

"Speaking about bringing them with us—I still have Alzy's playlist."

Oliwia raises her eyebrows. "That hard techno list?"

"That exact one. Want to listen?"

"The last time I listened to that—" She can't say it.

"Yes?"

"Lucija and I were getting ready in my bathroom. That's when you were attacked."

I swallow and take a deep breath. "Well, I'm still here and she's not. So how about some horribly misplaced Czech techno to scare off tourists?"

"Go for it."

I put on Alzy's list, and we both smile. It's *so* not the right time or place for it, which makes it perfect.

Chapter 16

OLIWIA

I might not have mentioned everything to Ing yet, but it's a start. Just us two admitting to each other we need comfort and support is like a massive weight off my shoulders. LeBeaux's words do still linger though. Wherever I am, whatever it is I am doing, I wonder what her real motives were. Surely it can't have been the fact that she was jealous of our wealth? And the "team"; what did she actually mean with that? Just the thought of there being more people behind all of what happened scares me beyond words, so I shrug it off the moment the questions pop up in my head for the millionth time. I'm not going to get answers to everything. Lebeaux is dead, decapitated by my girlfriend. Lucija is gone too, killed by me. Killer couple, the two of us. There's another box I won't open anytime soon. Neither her nor I have ever spoken about how we felt after having killed a human being. Not too sure about how humane they were, but they were still people—people that Karla and I offed.

"Ready, meladies?" Karel knocks on the toilet door. Poor guy has been waiting on us for a while now. Enough with the past, Oliwia. Not tonight. You'll have plenty of nights to think about back then. Now we're in Budapest, ready to go out.

"Coming!" Ingvild swings open to the door and jumps into Karel's arms. "So, what do you think?"

Karel is glowing with pride. "I can't believe you're my girl." He kisses her on the lips and twirls her around, her flowy summer dress and long blonde hair making fairy-like circles.

"Not too much then?" she asks, surely already knowing the answer.

"Never." He kisses her again, this time a bit more passionate and longer. Ingvild is never this affectionate in public, but behind closed doors, she's another person towards him.

Karla pinches my waist and whispers: "I can't with those two. The cutest."

Their energy lifts me up and properly catapults me back into the hotel room.

We've all made an actual effort, which is more than a welcome change. Ingvild in her long auburn dress, Karel in his summer shirt—with just enough buttons open for people to see his defined collar bone—and ripped jeans, Karla in her marine blue suit with cleavage I'm not mad at, and me in my neon green oversized t-shirt and short black shorts. I might not look as fancy as the other three, but it is still an effort. I look far more colourful than I feel on the inside, but it's time to loosen up.

There's a surge of electricity warping through the hotel room. We all look like superheroes. Okay, maybe a bit of a stretch, but let me have this moment. It's about time for a Polish superhero. I smile an actual smile.

"Let's do this!" I shout, and the others look up in confusion for a second and then shout back once they see my excitement.

"Are we walking or taking a metro?" Ing asks the rest of us.

I jump in: "Let's walk. It's a beautiful night, and we have over half an hour left before meeting the others. We can pass the Chain Bridge at night. It must be so pretty!"

Karel is blasting some Flemish electro music from his portable mini-speaker as we are all prancing down the road. We've never been this much of a unit. You can tell people around us are either annoyed by our rowdiness or semi-jealous of how well we gel. I'm proud of walking around with these three people next to me, so I pull back my shoulders and stand a little taller.

There it is: the Chain Bridge. We walk past the lion statues—a bit weird they don't have tongues; there's surely a story behind that that I will ask Karel about later—as the wind carried forth from the Danube embraces us gleefully. It's all a bit dramatic, and I am eating this up, all of it. The entire bridge is lit up with these sepia-toned lights, just like the Buda castle behind us. As we move towards the opposite end of the bridge, the Basilica and towering Parliament greet us with similarly warm lights. This city is magic at night. We continue our path past some gorgeous boulevards until we end up at the large square by the Ferris wheel. A tinge of anxiety tries to break through as I see how crowded this square is, but I won't allow it tonight. *You've fought for this, literally.* My stomach tenses up a bit as we slide past the many party goers all eager to get their pre-game on at the square. *You've got this, Liv.*

A hand touches my shoulder. I flip a switch and turn around, instantly grabbing the wrist as hard as I can, ready to fight.

"Hey, hey, chill! It's me!"

I look back.

It's Mihails.

Chapter 17

ANDREEA

I like this girl already. Nobody usually dares to mess with Mihails, but this Oliwia girl is not to be played with. I love that for her. She seems a bit stressed out though, but her girlfriend is hugging her, so she'll be fine.

"I told him not to be so rough," I joke, but it doesn't really land. "Anyway, good to see you all again. Come sit down with us. We were talking to some locals. They are super nice."

"Locals? Do you know them well?" Ingvild asks warily. These people need to lighten up a bit. I told Agueda they look posh. Maybe they're not used to hanging out outside in a square.

"No, we met them like ten minutes ago, but they are eager to practice their English."

There's an odd silence hanging in the air. Mihails continues: "Come on, then. We found a nice little spot next to a pond."

We all walk towards the pond and sit down with our new friends. I introduce them to the rest. "This is Balazs, and that's Szofi."

They all hug and kiss each other. The conversation starts flowing easily, and I must say, I might've been a tiny bit prejudiced. The four from Brussels are all smiles now. That's a bit of a relief; I can't deal with uptight people. Back in Romania, I probably wouldn't have even approached them, but Agueda was adamant about making new connections this trip. I count the nationalities around me in our circle of nine and I am pleased. That's what I came here for—mixing it up with other countries and cultures.

Balazs stands up and makes his way around the group. "So, is everyone up for trying a Fröccs?"

Karel replies, "A what now?"

"It's basically sparkling water with wine. You can choose what type of wine and the amount of alcohol in the drink. Want to come with me to order?"

"Sure, what can I get everyone?"

Karel and Balazs stand up and head off towards the summer bar as the rest of us continue getting to know each other.

Chapter 18

KAREL

I am glad Oliwia relaxed once she sat down. That was a bit of a rocky start to the night. None of us expected there to be more people, but then we've all gotten a bit rusty at this whole socialising thing. Balazs orders in Hungarian, and I try to understand what he's saying, but I can't—not even a word. Hungarian is a riddle to me.

"Can you say 'hello' in Hungarian? I need to learn at least some words while I'm here."

Balazs laughs, as I'm sure he's been asked this question a million times by lazy tourists like me who haven't studied the language enough.

"There are many ways to say it. The formal way would be 'jó napot kívánok'."

"Yo na what now?"

He cracks up. "You could also go for the shorter version 'jó napot'."

"Right, that I can manage, I think. What about the informal version?"

"That one depends on if it's singular or plural."

"You've got to be kidding me! How do you not get confused about your own language?"

"Well, we grew up with it."

"Makes sense. So, the informal one?"

"'Sziasztok' is like saying hi to a group of people and 'szia' means hey to just one person."

"Like the singer?"

"Come again?"

"You know, Chandelie-hier? Chandelie-hier?" I try and fail at my best falsetto. More laughs ensue.

"Exactly like that. How about hello in Belgian?"

"Eh, well—"

"Wait, wait, sorry. Belgian isn't a language, right?"

"Nope. Belgium is trilingual. There's the majority of the country that speaks Flemish - or Dutch—depends how you look at it—then there's French and German."

"German too? I didn't know about that one. Cool! So, which one do you speak?"

"All of them." I feel like a bit of a knob now. "You kind of have to if you live in a tiny country like ours. But Flemish is my mother tongue. And 'hello' is 'hallo.' Easier than your chandelier, isn't it?"

We walk back to our circle, drinks in hand, and continue our chat. Balazs is, as we say in Flemish, as tall as a door, with black curly hair down to his eyes. His posture is rather slight, oozing with kindness and warmth. Szofi also has curly black hair and is almost as tall as Balazs, so it doesn't take me long to discover they're brother and sister.

"So you two are siblings? And you go out together? That's really cool, dude. I've never had that kind of a bond with my brother," I say.

"Yes, Balazs and I are twins, actually."

"No way! So is it true what they say? Can you two—?"

"Read each other's minds? Hell no, I don't want to read my sister's filthy mind." He bursts out laughing.

I chime in: "Or the other way 'round, I'm sure."

Szofi smiles gently. "I might have a filthier mind than his."

That sentence has alarmed Oliwia. "What do you mean?"

Szofi forcefully takes Balazs' hands and shows the black ring on his right middle finger and the white one on his left middle finger. That only confuses me more.

Balazs loosens his hand from his sister's grip and takes over. "What she means to ever so eloquently say is that I'm ace."

"Ace as in great or ace as in greatly asexual?" Karla asks without hesitation.

"Asexual. Aroace, to be more precise."

I look back at Karla, hoping she will explain what that means before I look like the dumb straight guy who is still behind on all the queer vocabulary. Damn it, I thought I had made progress.

She picks up on my nervosity. "Aromantic, so you usually don't have romantic feelings for anyone, and you're not sexually attracted to them?" she replies, rather as a dictionary-like explanation to Dumbo over here than a reply to Balazs.

"Indeed, well, it's complicated to explain, seeing as it's such a spectrum."

"Totally, nobody is the same," Oliwia adds.

"Exactly. I mean, I have been in a platonic relationship once, but then I'm not sure if that was gender envy or a want to be close to that person just because I liked their presence and energy."

"But you don't have any sexual urges? Hope I'm not being too direct here, stop me if I am," Oliwia adds.

"I don't mind being open, hence the rings. I do have urges

at times. It depends on so many factors. Sometimes the mere thought of sex repulses me, other times I am in the mood if I know the person well enough and feel a proper connection. Does that make me demisexual or asexual? I'm not quite sure. I keep talking to people within the community, and it's still a bit of a learning curve. I wish I could put it more clearly, but that's me. A greatly asexual guy."

"One that I'm very proud of." Szofi beams with love for her twin brother and hugs him.

"I respect that you're so open about that to us, dude." My stomach sinks. "Is it okay to say 'dude?'"

Balazs cracks up. "Absolutely. Sorry, I didn't mean to be condescending. I know how much of a minefield it can be nowadays."

"Educate, don't cancel, I always say," Karla continues.

"Exactly! I hate that entire cancel culture. As long as people are open to learn, you can't expect everyone to know every single concept or word."

"Thank you!" I shout louder than I expected to. I can tell I'm going to like this guy. The rest of the group has been listening in, and I love the fact that nobody is making a big deal out of this. I know for a fact that my old friend group from some years ago in Brussels would've mocked the entire topic, so it's nice to see how chill the group is about all of this.

Balazs continues. "So, how do you four know each other?"

Ingvild is the first to reply. "We're all friends from school in Brussels. We go to the same boarding school."

"What's the name of the school?" Szofi asks. I wonder why she'd want to know those kind of details.

Ingvild hesitates for a second and looks at me for support. I nod at her—it's fine. "Europea."

Mihails frowns at the sound of that.

"Sounds serious," Agueda interjects.

The awkwardness hangs in the air.

"Right." I need to fill this silence. "Time for Palinka shots?"

Szofi nods proudly. "You've done well, tourist. Sure, I'll have a shot."

The second one follows shortly after, leaving me buzzed already. I'm not used to this magic potion. There are nine of us in a circle, but the conversation is split up into three groups because it is difficult to hear everyone in the middle of the crowded square.

"Everyone!" Andreea yells. "There's a lot of us here, so maybe we can make the rounds? Whoever knows the person next in line says some words describing them."

Feels a bit forced, perhaps, but not a bad idea for an ice breaker. I can tell this is not Ingvild's type of merry-go-round, but she politely agrees.

"Who's first?"

"You, since you suggested the game," Szofi replies, a little smirk on her face.

"Fine." She doesn't appear the least bit uncomfortable. I'm already anxious about my turn.

"Go for it then. Agueda, how would you describe me?"

The group is all ears. I'm actually quite intrigued now.

"Ha. Where do I start?" She pokes Andreea in her side.

"Be gentle, girl!"

"Fine, fine. So, Andreea in some words: charismatic, carefree, a dreamer. She's an extrovert too, in case you couldn't tell." We all laugh. This wasn't the worst idea after all. The alcohol is taking the edge off too. Mellowness is kicking in.

Andreea nods in agreement. "Anything you'd like to add,

Mihails?"

"She's Romanian, from Cluj. She studied cinema at university, and she's working on a pilot project for a Romanian series."

"Impressive!" She's got Oliwia intrigued now, another movie buff.

"Thanks, I'll send you all a link if it kicks off. Eventually. Next, Mihails! I'll go first." I'm not surprised.

"He's from a town near Riga in—"

"City." He's not too happy about that mix-up.

"City, excusez-moi, monsieur. I was going to say in Latvia. He is outspoken, a good planner, pragmatic. He likes the gym, in case you didn't notice."

We all noticed. Go ahead. Agueda takes over.

"He seems a bit tough on the outside, but he's a softy deep down." A nervous chuckle and blushing from muscle machine. That's nice to see, in all fairness. I might've been a bit judgmental.

"That'll be enough for now, thanks girls. So that leaves Agueda. Miss Portugal, from Porto, to be more precise. How could I possibly describe *you*?" He winks at her. Oh, there's some history between those two. Andreea pulls out a fake (I think, anyway) smile.

"Let's try. She works as a data analyst." That one I didn't expect. Neither did Karla. The large eyes she pops out make me smile, Miss Unfiltered. I thought she'd be an artist or something.

"She's also an avid basketball fan and player, character-wise. I'm bad at this. Andreea, help me out here?"

"Sure. Agueda is a planner as well I'd say, very giving and warm-hearted, sex positive. Is that a trait?"

Agueda cracks up. "It is in *my* book! Enough, enough. So, the Hungarians! This should be easy for you two, being twins and all."

The siblings exchange looks. "Want to go first, sis?"

"Okay. Balazs over here is brave as you've all just witnessed, kind, and as loyal as they come." This is sweet, a little sibling love in the midst of a drinking game. "He's a psychologist in the making, final year, and can read all your body languages in a second. I don't even try to hide anything from him anymore."

A part of me is creeped out by that, not too sure how much of my and the rest of the group's emotions I want him to read.

"Don't freak everyone out, sis." Exactly, thanks for reading my—oh crap. "So, Szofi here. She's a big reader, very family-oriented."

Szofi seems a bit wary about how open his description will be. There's a lot of communication happening between the two of them as we speak.

"She's into anime, comics, and true crime stuff."

"Might as well say 'she's a geek,' bro." We all laugh again.

"No, I don't mean any of that in a negative way. Why would I? She teaches me about these lores and multiverses all the time; it's really cool." No sarcasm or irony in his voice, good.

"That'll suffice then. That leaves—" She opens up the palm of her hand and elegantly directs the attention to us four.

Oliwia takes the lead. Ingvild and Karla both smile, like proud fans. "The Brussels gang. Let's start with—Karla. She's my girlfriend, so I might be slightly biased, but she's amazing." Melt. "Like you said about Balazs, Szofi, my girl here is incredibly loyal. Apart from being gorgeous, she'll win any debate any of you'd ever start. So don't even try." More smiles around the circle. "She's Austrian, from Innsbruck, but lives in Brussels like the rest of us. Karel is the only Belgian in the group, actually. What else—anyone?"

Might as well. "Karla is quite outdoorsy. I know she misses the Austrian mountains at times."

"True."

"And a great listener too."

Karla winks at me. "Why thank you, kind sir. Should I go for Karel then? Well, he loves a good political debate as much as I do, but he won't win them." Thanks. "Just messing. The biggest empath I've ever met, he's open to learning about everything. Also, a big history buff. And a planner. Seems like Agueda, Balazs, and Karel should plan the rest of our trip together."

Agueda interjects. "I want to hear from Ingvild, the girlfriend. What else should we know about your fella?"

I know this is outside of her comfort zone. She's been quiet so far. *You've got this, hon.*

"My fella? Spoiler alert, I'm not the best at these types of things."

"That's okay, love," Agueda says kindly.

"He's basically the most authentic, kind soul I've met in a guy. And he's sexy, look at that jawline." Oh, that Palinka is working wonders over there. Openly admitting she's attracted to me? In public?

"Now for my besty, Oliwia." She's not done yet either. That's my girl right there, people. "Ask her anything you want about superheroes. Szofi, you and she could have a geek off."

Szofi's eyes sparkle with intrigue. "It'd be my pleasure!"

"She's also very much into Cubist and Surrealist art." A second of silence. Oliwia shakes her head ever so slightly. She doesn't want the group to know about her horror knowledge.

74

I'm sure that's it. I slide in there to cut the silence short.

"Liv is Polish, by the way, from around Krakow. She is—as you can all tell—the one who makes connections very easily between people." She needs a little pick-me-up; no need to talk about how long ago it's been since her social days.

"Girlfriend!" Andreea shouts a little loudly. Palinka Effects 101. Karla is startled but complies.

"This girl here? The smartest, cutest Polish superhero of all times. Don't even try to convince me otherwise." I mean, come on now, cheese factory. But it's kind of cute.

Oliwia has had enough of the attention on her. "So, that leaves our Norwegian beauty, Ingvild."

"See, I *knew* she was Scandinavian!" Balazs says to Szofi.

"You guessed right, kind sir. Ing knows everything—and I mean *everything*—about architecture. She's mostly big on Art Nouveau."

The twins frown.

"Secession style here in Hungary," Ingvild explains.

"See what I mean? She even knows the names of the style in different countries around Europe. She is direct in the best way possible. She can pull the info she needs out of anyone. Not blunt, just to the point. A bit Dutch in that way, but smoother. Anything else?" She looks up at me.

"Oh right, the boyfriend should speak, I suppose."

"Yes!" Agueda replies enthusiastically.

"My Ing is intelligent, gentle, and a rock to everyone around her. She'll have your back."

Andreea and Agueda pull out an "Awww" at the same time.

"Well, that was nice," Szofi says. "Time for another shot?"

For some reason, we all agree.

The liquid burns down my throat, even with this being the

third shot. The supposed peach taste is barely there, the only thing masking how strong this is.

"Right, lovely people," I slur out. "Shall we head for the ruin bar? Instant is waiting for us."

Loud cheers of agreement burst out from everyone.

"If you can help me up, sure," Agueda says to Mihails.

"You're such a lightweight. Go on then."

We all stand up—some more easily so than others—and make our way to Instant.

Chapter 19

INGVILD

I haven't ever seen anything like this. After queuing up for a good twenty-odd minutes—good thing Mihails brought some drinks for the road—we enter what used to be a hospital. From the outside it looks like an abandoned, derelict Brutalist building, but once you step in, a whole delirium-esque world opens up to you. Room after room filled with all this quirky art, murals, bars, and plants. There's a lady walking around selling carrots in a little basket. In the room next to it there's a Hookah set up for whoever feels like smoking away whilst eating, eh, carrots. As you walk from one room to the next, the music playing from one DJ booth slowly meshes with the next one, each beat heavier and darker than the previous one. It's a delight to the senses in the weirdest of ways. Smoke, neon colours from old billboards hanging from the ceilings, rusty stairs filled with potted plants and flowers, and people. Sweaty, joyful, entranced people dancing to the beat of deep house and tropicana house everywhere. I almost walk into a room filled with TVs and cameras, but one of the bouncers steps in front of me and tells me this room is off-limits. Apparently, there will be a video installation performance in a little bit, projected in the other dance rooms. This entire place is a labyrinth, but somehow Balazs and Szofi flow through these rooms as if they've been here a thousand times. Then again, maybe they have. I would if I lived here. The effect of the pre-drinks together with the mishmash of stimuli around me takes me to a whole new level of excited. This place is a club, a gallery, a hospital, a carrot farm, all in one.

I check in with Oliwia. "Are you okay, Liv? This place is—a lot."

She kisses my cheek. "It is, but it is the perfect place to let go. I'm fine, boo, thanks for asking."

Mihails—who is looking damn good tonight with that tight white shirt on—yells at us. "More Palinka shots?"

We all agree.

The shots are working. A little too well. I haven't danced like this in years. Karla, Karel, Oliwia, and I all move to the intense beats without taking a single break. The others in the group are also going for it, although Mihails is a bit more composed than the rest of us. Now and then he sits down for a bit or talks to one of the girls around, but then he comes back and shows off some minimalist dance moves. Agueda and Andreea are like a unit, constantly hugging each other and jumping around. The twins glide from side to side and unite us all into one bigger group. My mind can finally switch off. Just music, movement, and fading away into the chaos of the rooms.

Agueda is dancing close to some random guy now, and the two of them seem to be hitting it off quite well. She knows how to flirt, that one. Good for her, I wish I were that confident on a night out. I shuffle next to Andreea and ask, "Is she okay with that guy?"

"Agueda? She always does this. I could use a bit of her

confidence. Don't worry about her—she is on the pull tonight. We usually lose her by the end of the night." She winks at me.

"Go girl. He's a looker alright."

"She always gets the hot ones. Not necessarily the nice ones though." Mihails is listening in to our conversation and looks perturbed.

I signal to him. "Is he okay? He seems a bit jealous."

"There's some history between the two of them. It's fine; he'll get over it."

The man pulls Agueda away, and as she jogs past me, she giggles into my ear. "I'll be right back. Don't wait up for me."

Chapter 20

AGUEDA

Where did he go? I swear to—This douche just pulled me into the toilet stall, and now he expects me to wait for him? I want to call out his name, but all of a sudden, I realise I haven't asked yet. Whoops. I smile to myself, sign of a good night. Maybe I'll wait one more minute. I mean he is almost as fine as Mihails, but I'm not going down that route again. It all got a bit too complicated with Andreea and him. I shouldn't have gone there again after they'd kissed.

Breath check—rank. I hope the guy is as far gone as I am. That's it, I'm out of here, back to the rest.

Oh, message? I thought there was no reception down here?

Unknown Number: *Told you we'd meet tonight.*

Hold on, what? I have completely forgotten to ask which one of the Belgians had texted me. Is one of them being flirty with me? I check and yup, it's a Belgian number. If this guy doesn't come back, I might as well have some fun with my new friends. I text back.

Agueda: *Which one of you is this?*

My heart starts racing. I love little games like these. A little bit of escapism never hurt anyone.

Unknown Number: *Go to the camera room next to the toilets. I'm waiting for you.*

The room that was off-limits? Kinky, I'm down.

I walk out of the toilet stall—well, I should say wobble. My mind's a bit blurry, and so is my vision. I can't tell if my head is thumping or if it's the loud bass from the dance rooms all around me. Okay, get it together girl. Let's see who's waiting for me.

I open the main door of the toilets and walk out. The camera room is right next to it. The bouncer isn't there anymore. Easy.

I walk in and skim the room. There are about twenty cameras and ten large microphones on poles set up in a circle. The room is mostly dark, with some occasional flashes of dark blue coming from the room next to it. The music playing next door is blaring loudly. On one of the TVs at the back end of the room, I can see myself walking towards the circle. Oh, this is trippy; I'm being filmed. I step into the middle of the circle.

"Hello? Which one of you is it?" No answer.

All of a sudden, the music next door changes into some psychedelic techno. Weird transition. I look back at the TV at the other side of the room and notice myself surrounded by colourful circles and 70s-themed patterns. I hear some voices coming from the dance floor. "Oh look, the video installation art has started! Look at that chick!"

It takes me a moment before it clicks. I'm in the video installation, standing in front of a green screen. How did one of the Belgians know? Is this some kind of a prank?

81

"Hello, who is doing this? Where are you?" I don't want to be the butt of someone else's joke, so I decide to leave.

Then someone shows up. I'm not sure whether this is all part of the installation or not, but the figure in front of me is wearing a creepy-as-hell mask. Kinky?

"Look, there's someone else in the video! It's totally avant-guarde!" Some obnoxious drunk yells from the other room.

The masked person walks towards me and pulls out the microphones from the poles.

"What is this? I don't get it. I'm not really into modern art, sorry." I try to stay calm, but something feels off here. Way off. It's too dark to tell what is happening. Is this the creep I keep seeing around?

Then it hits me. The poles. They are spears. Once the microphones are taken off, I can see them all around me, in a circle. About ten large spears.

"Wow, bro, this stuff is macabre!" There's that annoying voice again.

I need to get out of here. The figure is standing right in front of me in the middle of the circle. I am surrounded by the sharp spears, glistening menacingly at me. My palate dries up, and I am trying to swallow, but it's as if there is this massive lump stuck in my throat. Sweat starts trickling down my neck. What does he want from me? Maybe if I grab a spear and stab him, I can—

He jolts towards me faster than my reflexes can handle at the state that I'm in and stabs me in the foot with one of the spears. It penetrates my entire right foot. I look up at the video screen and doubt for a moment if I am losing it. This can't be real. Then the pain overtakes me. I scream my lungs out as I see the blood pouring out: "Help! Someone, help me!"

I hear more mumbling now coming from the dance floor next to me. Some girl is saying, "Damn, she's good."

The figure grabs another spear and stabs my left foot onto the ground. I am rendered immobile. I fling my arms around me with all my might, trying to hit whoever is behind that mask, but they're too fast. The figure ducks and takes another spear, this time piercing through my right forearm. I fall in and out of consciousness, trying to stay alert. I yell for help, but the crowd next door is starting to applaud.

"You freaks, this is real! I'm not acting; help me!"

Some people sound a bit more confused now.

"Is she okay?"

"Girl, are you okay?"

"This has to be fake, right?"

"A little intense for a night out?"

Another spear is jammed, this time through my left forearm. I am snapped out of my hazy state of mind and see everything with full clarity now, as much as that is possible. Four spears in my body. I feel weaker with each bated breath. I'm stuck. The masked man is standing opposite me again, holding two spears, one in each hand.

"Please, don't do this. I don't know why—" I try to continue talking, but I cough up blood. I inhale and try again, but I don't have enough strength left in me to speak. I need to speak though; that's all I can do. I need to get out of here.

"Mihails, Andreea, help me!" I yell with the last bits of power left in me. I exhale and lower my head. Why is he still standing there? I try to lift my head, but my neck muscles are shaking. My entire body trembles. It's about to give in. I can't give up though.

I see the mask approaching, tauntingly slow. Step by step.

Until it is right here. I can feel the warmth of this person's breath coming through the mask. I force myself to look up. The eyes behind the mask are pure evil, zero soul.

The figure lifts their arms and pierces the spears through my temples, one from each side. As I hear my skull crack from different sides, everything turns black. I hear some muffled echoes of people shouting in the distance.

The blades are here. There's no power left in me. Only cracking noises.

Chapter 21

SZOFI

I should've known better than mixing Fröccs with Palinka. Bad Hungarian. I feel a bit guilty that the entire group came outside with me when I vomited all over the curb, but I'm glad to get some fresh air. Balazs is holding my hair back. I am sweaty and start shivering when the wind hits my sleeveless top.

Some random girls run outside and start talking about how "disgusting that video installation was." Glad I missed it then. Good timing.

"You better now, sis?"

He holds me up and gives me a sweet hug. I love that he doesn't care how gross I am right now.

"I need a minute, but the air is helping. Thanks."

The others are looking at me with a mix of worry and pity in their eyes.

"I know how to make a first impression, don't I?"

The girls all laugh. Mihails, not so much. He is the more serious type, apparently. We lost him for a while when we were dancing, but he found his way back to the group.

"Can we do anything to help?" Ingvild walks towards me and strokes my clammy back. She retracts her hand a bit when she senses the cold sweat.

"I could actually do with some food."

"You sure that's a good idea?" she asks.

Balazs knows me well. "It usually helps her." They all look a bit puzzled. "It's not like this happens every week or month even, but I know my sister. Let's get some kebabs."

"Sorry about this, everyone. I'm really embarrassed."

Karla vehemently shrugs away that apology. "Don't be, seriously! We've all been there, girl. Food it is." She turns to Andreea. "Has Agueda messaged you?"

"No, actually. Mihails?"

He checks his messages. "Yup, she's texted me. She says not to wait up for her. She's off with that guy."

Oliwia looks distressed. "Will she be okay on her own?"

Mihails chuckles. "She is more than capable. She's a tough one. She said she'll be back tomorrow."

"Wait, what, so she's sleeping over at this guy's place?"

Mihails doesn't get the worry—I sense it. "So? We're on a holiday. She's free to do what she wants."

"Absolutely, I didn't mean it in a judgy way. I'm only a bit worried because she barely knows the guy. What if he's -?" She stops her sentence there and looks at Ingvild.

She takes over. "She'll be alright, Liv. Sorry, Mihails, we were trying to look out for all of you. No bad intentions here."

That has calmed him down, his body posture more relaxed. "I appreciate that. Thanks. We'll see her in the morning."

My stomach churns, the acid working its way up again. "Guys, I really need some food, like yesterday."

Karla lights up a cigarette and offers a drag to the others of her group, but they refuse. Her girlfriend definitely isn't too happy about her smoking. Complex bunch, those Brussels' people. There are some extra layers there, for sure.

We all walk off into the cobbled streets of District Seven.

Chapter 22

OLIWIA

The rude awakening of the chiming of the church bells next to our hotel warps me out of my nightmare. My head. I haven't had a hangover in a while. Now I remember why I barely drink. My throat feels itchy, and my forehead is rhythmically drumming into my skull. How is Karla sleeping through these bells? She will probably be even worse off than me. Today could be a bit of a challenge.

I stagger to my feet and open the velvet maroon curtains to see Pest in all its glory. I instantly feel better. A hangover is nothing compared to the stuff I've been going through. It's almost as if I'm living a normal life right now. This trip is a hundred percent helping. I might've been hesitant at first, but looking at the morning sun reflected in the Danube and the tourist ferries passing by in front of the balcony, I'm glad I took this massive step. Maybe it doesn't always have to be hard. Maybe it's okay to let loose and have fun again without the all-present guilt pushing down on me. It's odd—I don't feel too well, but my body is lighter. My shoulders are less tense, and I don't have to crack my back as much as I usually do.

Karla's loud breathing makes me look back at her. Those bleach blonde locks chaotically caressing her cheeks—I am still in awe of her beauty. I do not want to take it for granted. Ever. I decide today is a good day. We all deserve another good day.

A message comes in from Ingvild.

Ingvild: *Are you two up yet? Karel is off on his morning jog. Way too chipper. Breakfast?*

I didn't realise it is past eleven. My stomach is still quite full from that late night Turkish snack bar, but somehow I could eat again. There's another good sign. I'm actually hungry on this trip.

Oliwia: *I'll wake Karla up. Come over to our room. Let's order brekkie in bed?*

Ingvild: *On it!*

Chapter 23

INGVILD

Our lush breakfast is spread out over the queen-size bed. Fresh juice, fruits, granola, smoked cheese, croissants, you name it—it's all here. We went for the vegetarian mix, so Karla would have enough options too. Oliwia burps and is looking a bit worse for wear.

"You okay there?"

"Sorry about that, boo. Sure, it's helping, I can tell. Is Karel still on his morning run?"

"Yes, no idea where he finds the energy, but all the more respect to him. I couldn't do it this morning."

Karla lets out a large yawn.

"How about you, Karla? How are you feeling?"

"I probably didn't sleep enough."

Oliwia frowns her forehead. "You were deep asleep when I woke up though."

She stumbles on her words for some reason. "I—yes. I fell asleep quite late though."

"You usually fall asleep after me."

"Exactly." There's something unsaid there, but I won't go into it now.

I pick up where we left off yesterday. "Night two of partying tonight. Balazs said we could go to this big spa party with foam and stuff. Sounds fun, a bit '90s."

Karla cringes at the thought. "It could either be really fun or not my thing at all, but I'll keep an open mind. No drinking tonight though, I've had more than my share these last two days."

Oliwia and I agree. We often go out without drinking because we have some sober friends at Europea Halls, and it doesn't feel right getting off our heads with them around us. Detox day it is. I glance at my phone. "Strange, Karel should've been back by now."

A sudden pain hits the scar on my hand. I know what that means. I'm stressing out. Where is he?

Chapter 24

KAREL

I wasn't too sure when I woke up, but I'm glad I went on my run; I needed it. As I am jogging past the banks of the Danube, I spot some young families on the playgrounds around me. A couple of dogs are frolicking around, on the hunt for the largest branch they can find on the ground.

Jogging clears my mind. It's something I took up after the murders, and I haven't missed a single day since. I don't see why I should stop now. Some gorgeous villas pass my view as I run towards the bottom part of the gardens of the Buda Castle. The day-after effects are dissolving with each step.

Yesterday was fun, great fun actually. All these new people, that ruin bar, the four of us dancing—it made me feel grateful again. I want to hold onto that emotion with all my might, so I take in the sights around me and inhale the morning breeze.

No, not now. Those piercing eyes are burning in my neck again. I'm being watched. I'm sure of it this time. I spin around and scan every single face in my vicinity. It's not those two labradoodles, not the old ladies on the bench next to the gardens. Who is it? My chest cramps up, my breathing shallows. The melange of sport and angst sweat comes together on my forehead and a loose strand of hair sticks against it. I fix it and tighten my man bun, 'cause this I can fix at least.

There's no- one here. Well, nobody that looks suspicious or even remotely dangerous. I check my phone, half-expecting a message from an unknown number, but nothing. Oh crap, the time. I need to run back to the Hilton before Ingvild gets worried. I quickly text her.

Karel: *On my way back, lost track of time. Love you x*

Chapter 25

BALAZS

I slept on Szofi's couch last night, just to be sure she'd be alright. We both have our own place on the outskirts of Pest, but we often end up crashing at each other's. We were so burnt on being independent, but co-dependency is a thing among twins, let me tell you. At least for the two of us, I can't speak for everyone.

We grew up around lake Balaton with our mom. My biological father left us when he found out mom was getting twins, classy. I never missed a male figure in my life though, my mom's our rock. In retrospect I have no idea how she juggled a full-time job and raising twins. Szofi and I still go up to the lake every other weekend to hang out. My auntie lives there as well and it's a nice break from city life.

I haven't told my auntie about being aroace, but my mom does know and she acted exactly how I knew she would: with love and respect. I'm not sure aunt Aga would really get it, she's a bit more old-fashioned. I don't think she'd be against it, but I can't see her fully grasping it either. That's fine. I'm thankful my sis and mom are there to support me, because it's been quite the journey. Now that I'm twenty-two, I have the privilege to be surrounded by young, educated minds at university who don't have a problem with me, or my sexuality rather. In secondary school it was different though. I didn't have the vocabulary or the self-acceptance yet to even talk about rarely having sexual urges, but I knew I was different from all the other boys who couldn't stop sexualising every single topic we discussed. Everything - and I mean *everything* - on TV and the radio is about love, relationships, sex or break ups. It is so overwhelmingly alienating to grow up in a society that makes you feel like you don't belong, or you shouldn't. I only learned about amatonormativity two years ago, when I saw other aroace people post about the majority of society pushing long term, monogamous relationships as the only way to go. But that kind of vocab, ten years ago? No way. Even though I wasn't exactly bullied, because I somehow managed to remain semi-popular by playing football and the guitar - yes, the stereotypical activities *did* help- , I was extremely isolated on the inside. I couldn't tell anyone, because I didn't know what there *was* to tell. That's why I'm so glad and relieved in a way that there is a larger vocabulary on queer culture now. Many people - mostly online trolls - think it's a cry for attention or just say I'm emotionally stunted, but for me it gave my identity a home. A jargon I could rest my head against and know that it's not just me and there's nothing wrong with me. I have largely embraced my identity now, but there are still these pangs of anxiety that flutter up when I'm on a night out and someone starts flirting with me. I don't have the need to tell every random stranger who I am and what I stand for, but it still gives me the feeling of being cornered and that something is expected of me.

Szofi sits down next to me on the couch and exhales dramatically. I put my arm around her and she nestles against my chest.

"Still feeling rough I take it, sis?"

"Why do I do it to myself? No alcohol tonight."

"Agreed. It'll be nice just to hang out with that group from yesterday. We can swim around the outside pools, go to some Jacuzzis and saunas and have a good chat. I like them."

"Who?"

"All of them really. Good vibes from all of them. Can I ask you something though?"

She looks up and bites her lower lip. "What did I do wrong this time? Was I too direct again?"

"No, don't worry, none of that. I wonder - why did you show that much interest in their school?"

She leans back a second, gathering her thoughts. "Well, damn, of course you would've noticed that. Because - and I didn't want to say it in front of them - I know who they are. They look different, but the four of them together, the way they interacted."

"What do you mean? Have you met them before?"

"No, they're kind of famous in a dark way."

"Famous?"

"They are the survivors of the stabbings at that boarding school in Brussels."

"No way!"

"I know! That's why I asked for the name of the school, to be sure. Probably not the most subtle move on my part, but oh well. There was something about their faces that struck a chord. You know I watch too many true crime videos."

She really does. Like an obsession. "No comment. I had heard about that in the news, I had never seen their photos though. So, those people have lost all their friends?"

"Not all of them, but a lot, yeah. Crazy story. I am actually impressed by how open they were towards us. I'm not sure if I could trust anyone ever again."

"You'd have to at some point. It makes sense now though. I did notice that girl Oliwia being really tense when Mihails touched her."

"Yes! And then Karla was consoling and hugging her. At first I thought, oh great, another dramatic group."

"She was probably terrified, poor girl. Well, they handled themselves well, I can only respect them for picking up their lives again after all of that. But listen, sis?"

"Bro?"

"Let's not mention it to them. I'm sure they didn't come all the way to Budapest to be interviewed about past traumas."

"I'm not that thick! Of course I wouldn't."

I raise my left eyebrow and tilt my head at her.

"Fine, maybe I would've. But your gentle reminder works. I won't mention it."

"And don't go digging up dirt online now."

"Come on, you can't do that to me!"

"They're people Szofi, they've been through more than we can imagine."

"I hate it when you're the moral compass of the two of us. But you're right. Anyway, what time are we meeting up with them at Szechenyi?"

"We said to meet at ten in the evening at the main entrance."

"Cool, I wonder what they'll think about the spa."

"Tourists usually love it, don't they? I would. It's massive, I'm sure that Ingvild girl's mouth will drop when she sees the statues and buildings."

"Ah, she is the architecture buff, isn't she?"

97

"Yup, but I had the sense Karel was also really interested in the city. He did his research for sure."

"It's nice when people show interest, it always makes me feel proud of living in Budapest. "

"Same, it's nice to see people appreciate the beauty of Budapest."

"And its people." Szofi winks at me and gives me a hug.

Chapter 26

INGVILD

Today's the day we get our art fix. We first started walking around the Hungarian National Gallery, as they had an expo on Surrealism and then moved to district five on the Pest side to look at some small, quirky art galleries. Surrealism wasn't—or isn't—as big in Hungary as it is in Belgium, but here are some wonderful artists like Horna, Nemes, and Vacz that turned the movement into their own. Walking around the gallery, Oliwia and I lock arms whilst Karla and Karel are chatting away about politics again behind us. Not too sure they're very into this, but they promised us they'd try to show some interest.

Oliwia stops and freezes up. Oh no, the PTSD. What can I do to—? Oh, never mind. It's not an attack. She lifts her right index finger and points at the painting in front of her.

"Ing, look."

An emotional wave rushes through me. "It's a weeping willow."

"How coincidental. Our tree in a small Surrealist gallery. It's like we're meant to be here."

We hug each other tightly and forget about the others for a moment. Karla doesn't let us for too long though.

"What are you two being mushy about?"

99

Liv points at the painting, and to my surprise, Karla gets it straight away. "No way, a willow. Okay, that's very fair, keep hugging." She smiles as she pushes Liv and I closer together. Karel lights up as well, seeing me and Oliwia laughing and embracing each other.

After three galleries, we all felt rather exhausted and decided to head back to our hotel to have some rest before another night out. Luckily everyone is on the same page: sober night out this time around. I had to shake off the hangxiety a couple of times today, so I'm looking forward to some spa time.

Chapter 27

SZOFI

I haven't been to one of those spa parties in a while, so I decided on getting a new bikini. My other ones are pretty much worn out, and I want to make an effort tonight. Another hot flush creeps over me as I enter a way-too-hot clothing shop. Why do they have to make these shops so uncomfortable? Damn hangover.

I'll tell you, it's a big step for me, meeting all these new people. The pandemic has had its after-effects. I stayed in for two years, just this tiny bubble of mom, Balazs, and me. I haven't ever been the type to easily make new friends anyway, but the few times I've gone out since everything opened back up again have felt way different. I don't know if it's just my perspective, but people truly stick to their own friend groups, and it's as if that artificial bubble has continued on in clubs and bars. Before it was fairly easy to start a conversation with someone, at least local hungry tourists, but that's not the case anymore, hence the making an effort. I'm not entirely sure how much I can trust that group yet. I mean, there have been some pretty wild conspiracy theories online about Oliwia and Ingvild being the killers. Looking at them, however, you can tell they've been through the wringer. This unease they have around new people—at least we have that in common.

The shop isn't too crowded, luckily. Actually, there are only four other girls in here. The minimalist matte black bikini is winking at me. Guess I've found a winner. I glance around the shop. The changing rooms are all the way at the far left corner of the room. I brush past one of the girls and apologise for taking up too much space before I enter one of the fitting rooms and close the curtain behind me. You've got to be kidding me. Who ever thought these bright classroom lights were a good idea? I can see all my flaws, and today they stand out way more thanks to my dehydrated body. That reminds me—drink water.

I take the bottle from my purse and have some quick swigs. I breathe out; there we go, all is good. Balazs suggested a Palinka shot to feel better, but the entire Retox instead of Detox isn't my thing. I'll sweat it out instead. When I put the water back down in my purse, I see a person's shadow in front of the curtain.

"Excuse me, sorry" —how many ways are there to apologise? —"but this one's occupied."

The shadow doesn't move though, not an inch.

"I'm in here. There's another stall free next to me," I continue, scanning the shadow for any response, but nothing. My cheeks turn red, and the heat permeates through my entire body. What the heck is going on here? I take a prudent step towards the curtain and lower my view. Black shoes. They're kind of dirty and old-fashioned. Don't be too judgy, Szofi. I guess they do look a bit retro. Why aren't they leaving though?

The shadow takes a step closer, the cloth between us being the only thing that protects me. I look for a way out and notice the camera above me. I frantically wave at it and whisper "help" to it. Hopefully the shop keeper is being attentive. I'm not sure what is creepier, hoping the woman working here is looking at me in my underwear or this person in front of me standing there stoically. Perhaps I need to pull other people's attention. "Help! Somebody, there's someone harassing me!" I yell out at the top of my lungs. I hear some footsteps approaching from the other side of the shop. Hurry up, please, this is getting really freaky. Screw it, I'm not being caged in here. *Get it together, open the curtains.* My hands are trembling with fear, but I won't let some rando make me feel unsafe.

I fling open the curtain and notice a person wearing all black calmly walking away from me, hopping outside to the busy shopping street. Gone, just like that.

The girls in the shop meekly peek their heads out from behind the clothing railings, checking if I am okay.

Thanks for the help. See what I mean? It's everyone for themselves lately. Relief takes over and I sigh out a long exhale, the tension evaporating slower than I'd like. They should double check who they allow in clothing shops for women, seriously. I could use a Palinka shot right now.

Chapter 28

MIHAILS

I swear, that couple on the bunk next to us is going to need to have an IV of fresh saliva after the past few days. Gross.

"What did she write?" Andreea wonders.

"She said she'll meet us at Szechenyi tonight. She wants to join us for the spa party."

Andreea is visibly annoyed. "I get that she slept over at Mr. Hottie's, but couldn't she at least hang out with us during the day? We only have a couple of days together."

I have to agree with her. "I know. I'm not thrilled about it either, but what can we do? She said she would text me around eleven tonight."

"But you won't even have your phone on you; we'll be in a spa!"

"It's fine, I can go get my phone from the lockers."

"Not exactly ideal though, is it?"

"Not quite."

"So, dumb question maybe: but is it a naked spa?"

"No, most of the other ones around town are I read, but this one isn't."

"Good, I don't feel like shoving my breasts in people's faces." That idea excites me for a moment, but I decide to take the gentleman's route. "That would be awkward for sure." I check myself in the mirror, this t-shirt really shows off all the work I've been putting into the gym for the last months. Some might call it cocky. I call it confidence.

"Checking yourself out, are we?"

Damn, I'm caught. "Perhaps, fine, guilty." I turn red and look the other way. I catch a glimpse of the snoggers next to me and try to look elsewhere. I want to make sure I look good for spa night. I should do a couple of reps before going out tonight.

"Anyway, muscle man, should we head out for dinner?"

"Sure, let me quickly grab my wallet."

"Why, you buying?"

"Well, I can't *not* now, can I?" I teasingly reply.

Chapter 29

INGVILD

They keep throwing them at me, these awe-inspiring buildings. Even though we are ready for another night out—I can hear the electro swing blaring already—it is not the music I am focusing on, rather the neo-Baroque and neo-Renaissance facades of the baths that draw me in. The mild yellow tones together with the elegantly lit up statues are a sight to behold. I am getting my healthy dose of neo styles on this trip, can't complain.

Liv shuffles over to me, gently nudging my arm. "Are you sure about this?"

I instantly know what she is referring to. The scars. I've gotten used to people staring at my left hand, but I can usually hide the other stab wounds. I won't lie, I am uneasy about going out in public for the first time being so exposed, but I made a point to myself buying a bikini rather than a swimsuit before coming over to Budapest.

"I am. Nervous, but I'm sure."

"I get it." We both have stab wounds around our waist and stomach area, but it's dark out, and I'm sure the foam and what I am sure will be like stroboscope lights on acid will cover most of that up. It's yet another step in the right direction.

Entering the building, we see Andreea and Mihails waiting for us. The Hungarians haven't arrived yet. We greet each other and catch up a bit. Apparently, Agueda is still a no-show, but she'll join in later tonight. Those two do *not* look happy about that. There is a massive crowd inside the baths. I notice both Karel and Oliwia tensing up a bit.

"If it's too much, we can go somewhere quiet."

They don't want to hear that suggestion. Liv replies: "We've made it here, so let's just enjoy it. I mean, look at all of this!" She's right. We can see the outside pools with evaporating heated water being illuminated by the torchlights. The mythical statues stand tall and proud, looking over the party goers with a hint of disdain. The whirlpool on the left and Jacuzzis are packed full of people holding drinks in their hands. There's foam and tacky lighting everywhere. Karel told us this party happens once a month, they change up the water again right after. Good idea. I wouldn't want to go on a spa day where there are drinks, puke, and who knows what else still roaming about in the water. It's chaotic as hell out there. For a moment I think of getting a shot to calm down a bit, but being dehydrated in a spa full of strangers does not sound like a smart idea.

Liv pulls me closer. "But I wouldn't mind some quieter spots after tonight. You know, just to balance it out."

"I agree."

Once the twins have arrived, we all go to the lockers and get changed into our swimwear. No photos allowed on the premises, which I'm quite content with. I don't need some drunk stranger taking pics of me in my bikini. We walk outside to the party area and have a look at the map of the baths, hung up by the main door.

Karel scans a bit. "Right, so we are here, in front of the outside pools. There's an entire complex of inside pools and saunas too behind this bit. Do you all want to start inside or outside?"

It feels rather chilly, so we decide to head inside first. It's notably calmer there. We first enter a pool with hot water that for some reason turns my rings green. Sulfur, according to Balazs. The water comes directly from the springs, so they all have different healing properties. It's a magnificent sight yet again. The ceiling is covered with deep green shiny tiles that give the entire room an exotic touch. And low and behold: the patterns are Art Nouveau. I'm impressed yet again, Budapest, you haven't let me down yet.

We go from pool to pool, from sauna to sauna until we have kind of had it with going from cold showers to sweaty saunas. It's really good for your pores, sure, but exhausting too after a while. Because we are all a bit low on energy, we decide to head outside, 'cause the music and the party there will most likely wake us up. I take a big gulp of water—hydrate girl—and head outside, walking next to Andreea. She's been talking to me for a while about her hometown of Cluj Napoca, a really artsy city in Romania. She hasn't visited Brussels yet but is planning on doing so, or at least she says so. I do hope I'll see her again after the trip. I haven't made any new friends in a while, and I like how organically this is all going.

Once we hit the makeshift pool/dance floor, it doesn't take long for us to acclimatise. We don't really have the space or time to feel awkward 'cause there's so much happening around us. So I give into the music and dance in the water, foam floating between all of us, scars barely noticeable (I tell myself). The idea behind it is really fun, but there are so many creepy guys around, I'm not sure how long I'll last here tonight. I focus on Karel instead, who is looking mighty fine in his tight trunks, hair loose.

Something about this place doesn't convince me I'm safe here though. Smoke, foam, bright lights—there's so much going on that it'd be easy for anyone to lurk around here and hide, waiting to strike.

Chapter 30

MIHAILS

I am loving this. Wish we had parties like this in my city in Latvia, but I'll take it when I can get it. I'm subtly flexing my arms and chest as I'm dancing away to some deep beats, and I notice the stares I'm getting. Not just from girls either. I don't mind; look all you want boys.

"Question. How about another small game?" I ask the others after about an hour or so of dancing.

"I did this before in Barcelona with Agueda and Andreea. I admit, it's a bit geeky, but nice to learn about new cultures. So, give us three clichés—you know, like stereotypes—regarding your country that are at least a bit true." They all seem open to the idea.

"The country we're living in or our place of birth?" Karla asks.

"Let's say your place of birth, your motherland. I'll go first. I'm Latvian and three clichés would be that we all love singing and dancing. Fairly true. Second, we are shy and quiet. In public, I'd say so, at first. Last one, we're self-reliant and independent, heck yes."

"Cool, a bit similar to Polish culture perhaps then," Oliwia points out. "They say we don't smile a lot, true for some people in public, but different in private. We all supposedly eat fermented or pickled vegetables a lot. So true. And lastly, Polish people are hard workers. I can vouch for that."

Karla agrees as well. "Absolutely. Austrians. Tricky one, 'cause a lot of people mix us up with Germans. We're punctual people, very true. We have a quirky sense of humour, yup. And we all love the mountains. Maybe not all of us, but I definitely do."

A guy behind me splashes some water onto me and gives me a coy "oops" smile. Cheeky.

"Romanians next," Andreea continues. "First off, no, we're not all vampires unless you mess with us. I've heard from many visitors that we're hospitable, and I'd like to think we are. We supposedly are good at learning other languages. That one's largely true too, but not for everyone. A lot of Romanians speak many Latin languages like French and Italian 'cause they're related to ours."

"To latch onto the language thing," Karel states, "that one's similar for Belgians too. Our country is trilingual, so we grow up speaking three to four languages. Another one is that we're not easy to get to know. Sadly, that one is true as well, but we all say that once you make a Belgian friend, they're a friend for life. We're not flaky. One more? Flemish and Wallonians—the Dutch versus French speaking part—hate each other. Not true I hope. I have many friends from both parts of the country in Brussels. Let's just call it a bit of competitiveness between the regions."

"Now there's a euphemism." Ingvild cackles. "And you don't all eat waffles, fries, and chocolates every day either. That's mostly tourists. For Norway, some similarities with the Flemish. We're also a bit more reserved and like our own

111

space. We all eat salmon, depending on the region, but where I'm from, by the fjords, that's true. Eggs and fresh salmon for breakfast, yes, please!"

"That sounds delicious!" Szofi adds.

"Oh, it is! What else? We're all wealthy. A bit of an awkward one, but generally speaking, I'd say our average wage is far above most European countries." That one stings a bit, but she's not lying. The Baltics and Balkans can only dream of Scandinavian living standards, but things are evolving, luckily.

"Hungarians then?" Balazs asks us.

"Yes, please, we're in Hungary after all!" Andreea answers.

"Szofi, correct me if I'm wrong with any of these, yeah? We're all tall. A lot of Hungarian men definitely are."

"I mean, look at you!" Karla smiles. "How tall are you?"

"Almost two metres."

"That's crazy!"

"Yeah, but the tallest are Croatians and Bosnians, I think. The Dutch are pretty tall too, but Hungarians are usually more—what's the word? —broad-shouldered. Then, we're all pessimistic. I'm trying to break that one, but we often are regarding politics."

"No shame there, definitely the same in Poland!"

"Ah, really? Nice to know it's not only us. And last one. Szofi?"

"I'm thinking. That we're quite transparent and open, but avoid confrontation?"

"True, good one!"

The beat of the deep house track drops exactly at the right time. We organically move along to the beats. I love these little ways of getting to know new people. I always carry mindfulness cards with me in my backpack when I travel as well. If the conversation grows a bit stale at the hostel, I know what to do.

I look up at the big clock in the main hall and it's almost eleven. I should probably get out of the water and check my phone. Agueda better be on time; I'm not waiting around for her tonight. "I'll be right back everyone, going to check if Agueda has messaged me."

Half of them don't understand what I'm saying because of the loud music around, but Andreea has understood enough to roll her eyes. "Fine, be quick."

I walk towards the locker rooms. It's a bit confusing in here with all these numbers. The floor is quite slippery too. I brush past someone, and I feel something sharp touching me.

"What the—?" The figure is out of sight again. What was that? I look down at my belly, I mean six pack, and notice a tiny little wound. A drop of blood falls onto the floor. "Hey, twat, you cut me with something!" But there's no one around anymore, the entire room is empty. Who would wear all black to a pool party anyway? That was weird.

I unlock my phone screen and check for messages. At least she's punctual.

Agueda: *I'm here. Where are you?*

Mihails: *I'm by the locker rooms. Want me to pick you up?*

Agueda: *I have a better idea. Meet me at room 312 inside.*

Room 312? What is she on about? Is she flirting with me again? She has some explaining to do. What does she even mean

113

with room—oh right, the map. Let's have a look. I walk back towards the outside part, my stomach still a bit sore from that cut, and look for 312. On the inside to the right.

Mihails: *OK, I'll be right there. You're not supposed to have your phones inside btw.*

Agueda: *Live a little. Life's short.*

She's in one of those moods, I see. Not going to lie, she is turning me on a bit. I jolt past the crowd and put my phone back into the locker. I see the group dancing in the distance. Andreea gives me a "What's going on?" hand gesture, but I signal her I'm okay.

I'm back inside the bath complex. I should turn right. There, I see the signaling with all the numbers. It's becoming quite calm inside, not too many people about here. What is her plan this time?

312: here we are. Oh, she must've made a mistake or something. This room is off-limits it looks like. All I see in front of me is a dark small room with a—wait a minute, the Jacuzzi is turned on, but there's no one in here. How on earth did she pull this one off? I should've brought my phone with me. I'm too much of a goody two shoes when it comes to rules. I'm not too sure if I'm curious or scared, but I'd never say that to Agueda. She'd probably want me to get into the Jacuzzi, wouldn't she? I'm not too sure how Andreea would feel about all of this. I don't want her to end up being hurt again.

I close the door behind me —it's even darker in here now —and stretch my arms out in front of me so I don't bump into anything. The little cut in my abdomen is playing up again. It stings a bit, maybe not the best idea to get into the water, but I don't want to let Agueda down just because of a little wound. Screw it, I'm going in.

A rush of excitement shoots through me as I step into the hot, bubbly water. This feels amazing. I have a seat and go under completely, so my body adapts to the temperature. It's actually quite hot, a bit too much maybe. My breathing becomes shallower because of the heat.

"Agueda? Where are you? I'm in the Jacuzzi." I peruse the room, but it's hard to make out if anyone is actually in here. How did I put myself into this situation again? This will surely make it into my memoir one day.

"Agueda?" I'm starting to get a bit impatient and overheated, in more ways than one. I double check my pecks, yup, still looking sharp. A slight shuffling sound hits my ears from across the room. That must be her, playing coy.

"Ah, I hear you, no hiding from me. Did you miss me?" No reply though. I see, I am playing things by her rules. I can live with that. I change up my posture a bit, so I look as nonchalant as possible, making sure my arms are visible above the water line. The muted footsteps come a bit closer, still hiding in the shade of the room. I can tell she's on the left side corner. No fooling me.

All of a sudden, a phone is thrown at me and lands right next to the Jacuzzi. What is up with her? This is taking it a bit far. I filter the blackness of the room again, and I think I finally see a shape in front of me. I look back down and pick up the phone. There's a photo of Agueda on there, I think. It's a bit hard to see with the mist of the water clouding the space. I bring the screen closer to me to have a proper look at the photo.

It's Agueda, being pierced by what look like sticks all across her body.

She looks dead. There's blood all over her.

I hold my breath and frantically scan the room. Realisation gradually sets in. That shape is not Agueda. I've been lured into this room by whomever did this to her. Primal fear ignites in my entire system. I can't be next. I stand up to run out of the Jacuzzi when the figure in front of me steps closer, holding what looks to be a sickle. Hold on—the wound. This is the guy from before, dressed in all black. I jump out of the Jacuzzi to lunge towards the shape in front of me, but he lowers his posture. It's difficult to see in here, so I don't know where to aim for. The sickle slides deep into my abdomen, twisting the top end of it as it's cutting my insides. I let out a harrowing scream.

"You sick freak, what do you want?" This dude looks strong, but not as strong as I am. I move back, sliding the weapon out of me. It falls to the ground. I am trying to ignore the pain for now, and I start beating him in the face. I hear loud grunting. "You don't mess with me. Have you seen these guns?" I pound and push until the figure flops down onto the ground, twitching with pain. "Now what, you hero? Want a taste of your own medicine?" I pick up the sickle, but as I duck down, he trips me onto the slippery floor. *That pain, ignore it, come on, you're tougher than this.* I'm strong, but I'm not the fastest. I stand back up and so does he. Before I can make a move, the person in front of me is holding the sickle again, swooshing it towards me. I back off and miss the sharp edges by a centimetre. "Nice try!" I yell out triumphantly. This has triggered something in him, as the agitated movements inch closer and closer in a jerky fashion. The second he stops, I bolt towards the figure, push him onto the wall and strangle him. *Not me, you freak,*

116

you're not killing me. His entire body trembles now, trying to hold onto whatever oxygen is still left and swinging the sickle around, attempting to stab me. I'm not being killed, but I'll kill if I have to. I strengthen my grip and push down harder into the throat, being covered by the mask. I look into those eyes, but they're avoiding me. "Die!" I yell, frustrated and not understanding why he's not unconscious yet. The shape keeps flinging around his weapon until—

No. Hell no. The sickle is buried deep into my upper back. The torment too strong for me to hold onto his neck, I cry out in agony and release my grip. The figure inhales deeply, now glaring into my eyes as he slices down my back with the rounded blade as my arms flop sideways, too weak to hold onto him. I hear some cracking noises and the sound of blood spluttering onto the floor. I won't let him win, there's no way.

I recompose myself, even though my eyesight is fading, and hook him in the face with my right hand. Another loud grunt. That has slowed him down.

Run, now.

I swing open the door and look out into a dark hallway, the only lights coming from the party outside. The figure is right behind me, trying to cut me up even further, but not hitting the spot this time. I stumble forward into another off-limits room. It's a small sauna. I hold onto the wooden door frame in order not to fall down, but the sickle carves its way into my right hand the moment I do so. More agony pierces through me. My vision is becoming blurrier by the second, sweat dripping off my buzz cut straight onto my forehead and lips. The salty taste reminds me I'm still here.

Fight. *You've got this man.* The shape pulls out the sickle and shoves me into the sauna, closing the sauna door and locking it as I drop down onto the floor. What is he—? Oh, no way.

He turns on the controller next to the sauna room, and I can see him setting the temperature to maximum. I pound on the wooden doors, trying to get out, but the pain in my hand is excruciating. "Help, someone! I'm stuck, help!" That one hurts even more. I hate asking for help. I catch a tear rolling down my right cheek.

I can't die like this.

I pound the door with my left hand, but the intensity lessens as the heat of the small room scorches through me. It's hard to breathe in here. "Let me out, please! Leave Andreea alone, you hear me?" It's not mere sweat I taste anymore. There's blood too. My entire body is bleeding out, looking far too red from the heat. I can't hear nor see the figure anymore. I'm left here on my own. Okay, slow down, you need to save your—I can't—I try to exhale slowly, but my vision is almost entirely gone. The flesh on my body tightens and I am scared it will crack. I need to—breathe—you—breathe.

Chapter 31

ANDREEA

I'm a fan of this Ingvild girl. Of all of them really. They've been so nice to me the entire night. I can't help but feel jealous though. Mihails has been away for a while. I swear, if he's hooking up with Agueda again—don't go there. They're probably just catching up. It's been over half an hour though.

I stop Ingvild mid-sentence. "Sorry, but I'm going to go to the toilets and have a look where Mihails is."

"Oh, sure, do you want me to go with you?"

I ponder on that one for a second, but I want to talk to him on my own. "I appreciate it, but I'll be fine."

I step outside of the heated pool water, and the cool breeze is far colder than I'd imagined. The rest of the group continues dancing and waves at me. I give a little wave back. I head back into the main entrance and make my way down to the lockers. Which way was it again? There are people everywhere here, mostly making out. I slide past what appears to be lovers' lane until I can find my locker. Finally. I unlock its door and snatch my mobile. He has texted me.

Mihails: *Agueda is feeling sick. I took her to the hostel. Come?*

Nice. She's finally back and then she spoils the night out as well. I'm having a good time here though, but those two are still my friends.

Andreea: *Fine. Be there in 30.*

I hurriedly walk towards the group to tell them about Agueda. Ingvild and Oliwia are visibly disappointed.

"Are you sure you don't want to hang with us?" Oliwia wonders.

"I appreciate it, but they're my friends; I can't ditch them." *Like Agueda did*, I add in my head.

"That's nice of you." She smiles kindly.

"Will you join us tomorrow for tea at New York Cafe?" Szofi eagerly asks. She has just come back from some time out on the loungers inside. I guess she needed a little break from the crowd.

"That posh place? Sounds like a bit of me." I kid. "Sure, what time?"

"Say four?"

"Perfect. We won't be able to stay long though. Our ferry back is at seven."

"Can't believe how fast time flies sometimes," Balazs dolefully says.

"I know. It's all going a bit too fast for my liking too. I'll text you all later. I'd give you kisses, but you look sweaty."

Karla appears to be a bit self-conscious but then realises I am messing with them.

They all shout, "See you tomorrow!" before I make my way towards the changing rooms.

I shut the main door behind me and head towards the hostel. It's not that much of a walk, but it's darker than I'd like. Mihails could've at least come and picked me up. He'll never know what it's like for a girl to walk alone at night in a big city. Budapest might be all gorgeous and whatnot during the day, but there's something eerie about these dimly lit side streets at night. I check my Google Maps so I can take the big boulevards instead; there'll be more people on those roads. I change routes and immediately feel safer. There are plenty of people strolling about, some more boisterous than others. I'm glad I took this route.

I am about to put on my headphones when I notice it. Someone dressed in all black staring at me from the other side of the road. Instant stress—it's that creep Agueda was talking about. I'm sure it is. Is he wearing a mask? Some people bump into the guy and shout, "What's up with the mask, dude? It's not Halloween yet!" before continuing down their wobbly steps. That's it? They're not even a bit scared? Screw this, I'm picking up my pace. Breathe from the belly, deep breaths, you're fine.

My tread a bit faster, I look straight ahead and focus on getting back as soon as possible. I am supposed to continue down the boulevard, but I know the seventh district well enough by now to know I can turn down a street and then walk parallel to ditch that creep. I turn right and head into a small side street. There's nobody else here. Maybe not the best idea, Andreea. Come on girl, you're more street smart than that. I should've stuck to the boulevard. I tilt my head back and notice the creep has followed me here. My heart stops for a split second.

This can't be good.

Walk faster, it's not far now. I don't want to look back, 'cause then he'll know I'm scared. Shitless. I feel him moving closer, go faster, come on. I can't resist the urge to look back and see how close he's gotten.

"Stay away, creep! I'm calling the police on your ass!" But he just continues in a steady, stoic pace. It doesn't even look like he's rushing, just gliding past the pavement without any sign of fear or hesitance. I want to call the police, but I might lose too much time. *Just get to the hostel first.* One more street. I think. I feel a hand gliding down my back, caressing me in the creepiest of ways.

"Keep your hands off me!" I turn back once again and slap him hard in the face, or mask, rather. I don't wait for a reaction but run down another small road that leads to the hostel. Damn, he's running as well now. I pick up the pace but realise he's catching up on me. Almost there—I can see it from here. He's closing the distance between us. I run past a red traffic light. I couldn't care less about being a good citizen right now. A car flies past right behind me, lengthening the distance between the creep and me.

This is it—my chance for a way out.

I run as fast as I can towards the hostel, glancing back—I don't see him anymore—open the door and smash it closed. The young girl at the reception desk looks scared. There's no one else here besides her and me. I run up to her and scream: "Call the police, now! I'm being attacked!"

"What? Are you sure?"

"Are you really questioning me if I'm—? Yes, I'm sure. Don't let anyone in here. I was being followed. I need to find my friends."

She stumbles over her words. "So what—do I need to—?"

"Do your goddamn job and ring the police!"

I sprint up to the second floor of the hostel and enter our room. An awful smell hits my nostrils. Nobody here either? Not even the snoggers? I guess everyone's going out at this time. I need to find Mihails and Agueda ASAP. Then I see it. Of course. The two of them are lying next to each other, spooning on the top bunk. Deep asleep by the looks of it. I don't care, they ditched me, I need them right now.

"Mihails, Agueda, wake up! I was being followed here." No reaction. Really? Come on now guys. "I said wake up." I push onto Mihails' arm, noticing the bed sheets are clammy. How did that happen? As my eyes adjust to the darkness of the room, I think I spot some weird stains on the bed sheets. I instinctively go for the flashlight of my phone and turn it towards them. I scream and fall down. I see their bloodied, dead bodies, all carved up. Mihails looks burnt to death and Agueda's face—I can barely recognise her. This creep, it's this creep. He's a killer. I'm the only one left here, my friends are—gone. Isolation and anxiety in their purest form invade me. I need to get out of here. The throbbing pulse in my forehead makes me slow down. *Stand up, you need to get out.* I pull it together and stand up. Then I hear a horrific scream coming from the ground floor. The receptionist. Oh my God, he's inside. *He's here.* I can't make it to the front desk and run out, he's over there. I bolt towards the window, open it and peer down. Higher than I thought for the second floor. What else can—I—? The rooftop bar, there must be people there. I hurry to the door and quickly open it.

He's here. Right here, next to me. I let out an intense scream. He's carrying a bloodied sickle. That poor girl. The mask looks messy and stained, with hints of dried up blood. He lifts his arm and sickle, but I'm way ahead of him. I rush towards the end of the hallway. "Help, somebody! There's a killer here, help!"

One tourist shouts back from behind a door: "We're trying to sleep, bitch!"

I want to start an argument, but time and place. The lift at the end of the corridor is closed, so I opt for the stairs. No time to waste. As I start my way up, the figure is right behind me. *Keep a steady pace. Use your gym practice.* Two floors up and I can get help. I hear the sound of the sickle breaking through the air, barely missing my back. "Leave me alone!" I'm not looking back this time. There, almost.

Third floor.

Okay, keep at it. Go. I lift myself up with the railing of the stairs, but the figure smashes his weapon into it, right next to my hand. I'm lucky.

Okay, one more floor.

Steady breath, that's it.

Third time's a charm. The sickle cuts into the back of my neck. My long hair takes some of the impact, but I've definitely been hit. It hurts like hell. I lose my balance and almost fall down, but I'm still on my knees at least. Another slash, this time in my back. I see the entrance to the rooftop just some metres away from me. *Stand up, stand up.* I kick the figure down a couple of steps with my right foot, making some room for escape. I bite through the discomfort and make it to the landing. There's someone inside. I'm not alone anymore. I open the glass door that leads into the covered part of the rooftop and see a bartender.

"Miss, we're closed . I—" He stops and looks at the state I'm in. Then he takes a step back and sees my wounds. "What happened?"

"Lock the door, there's a killer!" He rushes to the glass door without hesitation, but it's too late. The killer is facing him and with one swift move slashes his throat left to right. I only see the back of the bartender, but I notice enough blood splashing into the air to know.

My heart sinks. I'm alone again. On top of a building. Dumb move, such a dumb move. I run further along the rooftop bar to the uncovered part, the wind warning me. The killer is disposing of the body, dropping it to the side, and he makes his way over to me. Calmly this time. There's no haste. Calculated, confident steps. I look over the ledge. I'm up way too high to survive a jump. The people on the street look tiny. The other buildings next to it aren't nearly as high, so I can't jump onto another rooftop either.

This is a dead end.

"Stay away from me! What do you want from us?" The figure steps closer and closer. I'm standing by the ledge, nowhere to go. I could let him get as near as possible and shove him off the building or go down and run past him. I've got options. This doesn't have to be the end. *Let him come to you. Get ready.* He continues his path, just a couple of steps now.

There. A mere couple of steps away from me. *Keep your balance, stand tall, you can go to a hospital right after this.* But instead, I cry. It's too intense. Too final. He lifts the sickle sickeningly slow, this is it. I push onto his chest with both hands and try to move past, but he pulls my hair from the back and holds onto it.

"Let go!" I scream, hitting him with my elbows, but I don't have enough strength left. The smell of blood hits my nostrils. I forgot about the stab wounds for a second. I stomp my left foot into his knee, and we both fall onto the floor, him on top

125

of me. I try to wrestle my way out of his grip, but he's holding me down, pushing his hands onto my shoulders, sickle at the ready. I sob, feeling utterly deflated.

"Do it, just do it!" I yell at the killer. I can't do it anymore. I have no muscle power left in me. Then I see those eyes. Is there hesitation? Fear? Pity, perhaps? There is a person behind this mask. I change tactics.

"Let me live, please. You've already killed my friends." Taking advantage of this momentary lapse of speed, I head bump him as hard as possible. As he takes his hands to soften the blow, I roll out from under him, pushing the heavy body to the side. I stand up, wobbly, imbalanced, but I'm up.

I exhale and ground myself. *Run down, now.* When I look back at him, he's up again too, facing me. Suddenly, I hear a loud car siren blaring into the distance—it distracts me for a split second.

I glance back and see the sickle bearing its way down into my neck.

He's got me.

I want to cry for help, but I know this is it. There's nothing else I can do. I feel the blade cutting through my neck, crushing my last bit of hope. The gaping wound making it impossible to breathe, my eyes roll up. I can't see anymore, but I feel him pushing me off the ledge.

I think I'm falling. I'm dying.

The wind bursts through me, breaking me.

Chapter 32

OLIWIA

I have to hand it to Ingvild; she knows how to pick the nicest places in the city. Karel was a bit sullen that he hadn't thought of this in his planning, but apparently New York Cafe has been voted as the most beautiful cafe in the world countless times. I can see why. I won't be able to describe it as elegantly as Ingvild, but there's basically golden and pink twirling columns around us everywhere. The painted cherubs on the ceiling remind me a bit of Alzbeta's home. They always creeped us all out. Here it works though. The four of us have taken a seat, which Ingvild had reserved. Good thing because there was a massive queue at the entrance. She made sure we got a nice little tucked away table, hidden from the crowd. Mihails, Agueda, and Andreea have canceled on us. Apparently, Agueda got really sick, and they had to take an early ferry home. Something about that feels off though. I'm probably over-analysing again, but why couldn't the other two come over? Is she really that sick, or was there some drama between those three we weren't aware of? The Hungarians are on their way over.

"So you think they fell out?" Karla asks me.

"I'm honestly not sure. Don't you think it's a drastic move to change ferry tickets instead of her sticking it out in the hostel until it's time for the ferry? They were leaving today anyway."

"There was tension between them, that I did feel," Karel interjects. "Andreea didn't seem too happy about Mihails trailing off to find Agueda."

Ingvild smirks. "I love how you pick up on stuff like that. A lot of guys wouldn't."

"Don't you even say 'one of the girls' Karla, I swear."

"Hey, I didn't! Haven't you noticed I've become a beam of lightness and joy around you?"

He cackles. "You sure have. Anyway, I think there was some strange triangle situation going on with the three of them."

"You reckon?" I thought so too, but I didn't want to sound narrow-minded. "Nothing wrong with that, as long as they all agree with the boundaries and—"

"They didn't though," Ing interrupts. "They didn't agree; you could tell."

We can see the Hungarians making their way over to the table. Balazs is impressed. "How did you get a table at this side of the cafe?"

"Hello to you too," Ingvild says, kissing both him and Szofi, and continues. "I have my ways."

Szofi looks uncomfortable. "I've never been to this side."

"The dark side?" I grin.

"The posh side."

None of us four know how to react. Sometimes we're a little bit too blissfully unaware of our privileges.

Ingvild cuts through the silence. "So, everyone up for some high tea?"

I hear a ping sound coming from Ingvild's phone, Karla's too.

Karel's and my phone buzz. All four at the same time. Fear grips me. Instantly.

Balazs smiles. "Group chat?"

My heart races. "No, no. We don't like group chats."

"Why?"

"Eh, I—one second."

All four of us look at each other in panic. I take out my phone.

Unknown Number: *Ask the Hungarians to check the local news.*

I show my message to the others. They have all received the same message. Karla instantaneously reaches for my hand and squeezes it. There's no way. Please let this be a prank. Please.

The twins look scared. Szofi goes first: "What's going on? You all look terrified."

Her brother continues: "Can we do anything? What happened?"

Karel exhales, pursing his lips. "Could I ask you to-to check the news?"

Balazs stammers. "The news? Like, which channel?"

"The local news, from Budapest."

The twins look at each other in distrust. They both open their phones and scroll through the news. I can feel a PTSD attack setting on. The noises start fading, the colours turning grey. My palms are sweaty, and my shoulders stiffen. My breathing becomes irregular.

"Hurry please," I whisper.

Ingvild sees me from across the table and makes an *Are you okay?* face.

I go "*No.*"

The twins are shocked. Absolute horror on their faces. They

129

exchange glances and show each other their screens.

"Please hurry." The sound is echoing stronger in my head.

There's ringing in my ears now too. I know what this means.

Szofi talks in a grave, serene voice. "The hostel. Andreea, Agueda, Mihails, and two other people were murdered there last night."

Everything fades away.

Chapter 33

INGVILD

"Get a waiter, now!" I shout to Balazs.

"What for?"

"Ask for ice cubes. Hurry!" He looks at Oliwia and then back at me with clearly no idea what is happening and scurries off. Liv 's having an attack. She's in freeze. Her entire body frozen, her eyes not reacting to anything. Szofi is horrified by the sight of it.

"Does this happen often?"

"She's got PTSD. She needs ice cubes to shock her nervous system. Karla, keep talking to her."

"I'm on it," she replies, gently whispering into Oliwia's ears. No response whatsoever though.

Somehow, focusing on Oliwia's state counterbalances my own initial reaction of total fear. I can't control what happened yesterday, but I can help my friend right now.

The waiter and Balazs come back, handing over some ridiculously posh ice cubes —in the shape of stars—really?—to me. I wrap a napkin around them and push it into Liv's hands.

She is coming back. Slowly, but I see a reaction in her eyes. It will take some time, but we've been here before. I know how this works by now.

"You're safe Livvy, you're with me. Ingvild and Karel are here too; we're all together in here. You can come back to us. We won't hurt you. We all love you."

Tears roll down my face as I see Karla's kindness, this pure and calm, in front of me. She's crying too. She wipes the teardrops away so Oliwia won't notice when she comes back, but this breaks her heart too. This *cannot* be happening again. Focus on Liv first. One thing at a time.

Oliwia is sobbing into Karla's arms. She's back, but the realisation is kicking in hard. The twins sit there as if they've seen a ghost. Balazs pokes me. "You need to tell us what is happening here. I mean, I know it's horrible what happened, but why are your reactions so intense?"

Szofi responds. "You know why, bro. I told you."

His eyes open up wide. "Is this connected? The massacre in Brussels?"

The last thing I want to do is tell them the entire story right now, but we owe it to them.

Someone needs to tell them to close their mouths. As in, now. They kind of knew the story, but they heard the story from the media's perspective. They didn't know our experience. Oliwia has been sobbing the entire time whilst Karel and I have been— as coherently as possible—retelling our stories. It still cuts deep, talking about losing our friends. But there's an added layer of fear sprinkled on top of it now.

Szofi is trying to understand everything. "So this means Balazs and I are in danger too now?"

"I don't know, Szofi. I can't promise anything."

"What kind of an answer is that? Bro, we need to go to the

police right now."

Oliwia springs up. "No! They didn't do anything last time to help us, and I don't trust them. One of the killers was a detective. There could be an entire unit that was working for her. Listen to me carefully. Do *not* go to the police." Her eyes are piercing through Szofi's. She swallows.

"So what are we supposed to do instead? I'm sure they'll contact us soon. We all went out two nights in a row—we're all over their socials."

"Go home. Go far away. Get out of Budapest now." Liv is deadly serious. "The longer you wait, the higher the chance you'll get killed. I need you to trust me on this. Get out of Hungary. Do you have a car?"

Balazs nods his head. "We came by car, yeah. But maybe it's safer to stick together?"

Karla chimes in. "No. You're not safe around us. Nobody is." That hits home. She's right though. They need to leave.

The twins stand, in total disbelief of the entire situation. "Let me text you at least."

Karel responds this time. "Only if you need help or something bad is up. If you're safe, don't text us. Not until all of this is over. So sorry you got dragged into this, genuinely, but Oliwia is right. You need to leave."

Before saying anything else, the twins hug us all and run away, out of sight. I hope that's enough. I hope we have saved at least these two people.

The four of us sit at the table, not sure what to say or how to act. All of us are processing the news in our own way.

"What if that was a mistake?" Karla throws in the group.

"How so, boo?"

"What if one of them or both of them are the killers? Wouldn't it be better if they were around us at all times?"

"Keep your friends close, your enemies closer," Karel adds.

"Exactly that! Now if they are guilty, we've given them the green light to roam about the city, stalking us."

I disagree. "No."

"No?"

"No, Karla. They came across as genuinely nice people. If we have the slightest chance of saving people around us, that's what we need to do."

Karla isn't convinced though. "Nice people, you say? Didn't we all think Lucija was nice? By the way, how did we get that message about 'the Hungarians' the exact moment they sat down?"

A growing sensation of unease sits in the pit of my stomach.

"That means whoever sent this can see us. We need to get out of here. Now."

We all get another message. The fear spikes up again.

Unknown Number: *KOIK*

Chapter 34

OLIWIA

The waiter kicked us out the moment Karel and Karla started running around New York Cafe, looking for a sign of the killer. Well, looking and shouting. They weren't exactly being subtle about it, but I appreciate them trying to find out who is doing this to us, again. We took a bus ride back to the hotel, which felt like a far longer journey than it usually does. We all remained quiet, squinting our eyes trying to find someone suspicious in the bus or on the streets. Nothing though. A state of limbo—in between places, trying to sort out my emotions, trying to stay grounded. The ugly truth is setting in. This was never going be to over.

And now here we are, back in the hotel. The four of us are all seated in a circle on the queen-size bed in Karla's and my room. The four of us, turned into a deadly acronym. Deep down I knew it was bound to happen again, LeBeaux's comment about her "team" sneering in my ear drum.

"I am going to ask you something you won't like, Livvy."

I swallow hard and stretch my spine. Multiple vertebrae crack away the tension. "What is it?"

"We need your slasher knowledge."

The Slasher Box. Pandora's seems way more tempting to open right now than that one.

"What do you mean?"

"You know what I mean. We need to talk about this."

Karel and Ingvild both bite their lower lips, impatient for my reply.

An odd sense of calm resides in me now. "What do you want to know?"

Karla looks at the others and then turns her attention back to me. "Are the rules different this time around?"

I know what she is trying to word. "This time around, meaning, a sequel?"

"Yes, a sequel."

The four of us exchange knowing glances. Ing and Karel move a bit closer to us, Ing lowering her back, eager to learn. Here I go then.

"There are many rules to slasher sequels, but it depends if we're looking at the original rules or the post-modern ones." There it is, rolling out of me the way it used to. The smell of the gluten-free bagel with cream cheese in our Brussels' hub permeates through my memory, throwing me back into our corner. Marieke, Lucija, Ingvild, and I discussing slasher rules. Ayat and Alzbeta had already been killed at that point.

"Tell us whatever you can," Ingvild suggests.

"Right, let's start with the basics. There are some cliches often used in sequels, such as a higher body count, more elaborate death scenes, killing one of the survivors of the original. It's all discussed in Scream 2 with that Randy and Dewey scene." They all know the one I'm on about.

"But not you," Karla claims. "You were the Final Girl in the first movie. You'd be slasher royalty by this point."

I hesitate. "Well, Wes Craven definitely never wanted Sidney to die, that's true. But that's where I'm not so sure. I almost died. Lucija would've been the Final Girl."

"Or LeBeaux," Karel mutters.

"Right, the Final Woman or whatever. Sequels are often a bit longer too than the original, more of a buildup."

"Mihails, Agueda, and Andreea as opening kills?" Ingvild wonders.

"Maybe. Unless they were fake-out deaths."

"Fake out?" Ing questions.

"In some more recent slashers—well, I don't know how it has evolved over the past year and a half; I haven't watched any— there have been 'fake' deaths, later turning out to be the killer."

Karla pulls a disgusted face. "I don't think that's the case for those three. I don't mean to be too morbid here, but from what I saw on the news report, those three were not just killed. They were slaughtered."

That confuses me a bit. "Okay, so maybe no fake-out deaths."

"So who usually survives then? The main cast bar one?" she asks, her eyes full of worry.

"It really depends. Usually, one or two of the new cast and then the originals."

"Who would die of the original cast?" Ingvild interrupts.

"I mean, the one that'd hurt the most to the Final Girl and the audience."

"Me? The best friend?"

I hope to whatever it is I still believe in, that won't be the case. "I hope not, Ing."

"What about us two, Livvy?"

I'm not too sure there. "It depends on that entire 'bury your gays' Hollywood trope."

Ingvild and Karel's body language give away they need a bit of an explanation.

"It's the idea that the audience wouldn't be too interested in gay side characters, so after some sort of melodramatic scene, they'd be killed off. Or if there's a queer or queer-coded couple, one of the two would die, meaning no happy ending ever for the gays."

"I'll probably sound dumb, but I thought it was 'kill your darlings,' that trope? Or 'murder your darlings'?" Ing ponders.

"No, that one means a writer edits out his favourite parts or something? I'm not sure. Speaking of murder, that brings us to the suspect list. Bigger cast means more guessing work. Let's start with the Hungarians."

Karla jumps up. "Them! They knew about us, about our past."

Karel isn't convinced. "But then who doesn't? It was all over the news in Europe; maybe they put two and two together when Ing said we go to Europea."

"Aha! There's another thing! Why was that Szofi girl so interested in which boarding school we go to? She'd barely met us. And she likes true crime podcasts, apparently."

Ingvild snickers. "Who doesn't these days?"

I try to rein in the stream of consciousness around me. "So, Szofi. We don't know much about her except for her showing interest in us and her love for true crime. Could be her, sure, but it seems obvious."

"The brother?" Karel lifts his left eyebrow.

"Balazs? Well, everyone's a suspect. So why wouldn't he

be?"

"He seems like such a nice guy though. Really close to his sister, welcoming us to the city, showing us around Instant. I can't imagine—"

This time I am the one cutting him off. "Maybe he is just kind of positioning himself at the background as the nice new guy. Or it's the two of them together. Twin killers. That's a fresh idea."

Ingvild scratches her forehead. "What would their motives be though? They don't like tourists?"

A silence washes over the bed, none of us knowing how to answer that one.

I gather my thoughts. "Maybe they have a connection to LeBeaux. There's another thing we have to discuss, everyone. If this is a sequel, there must be some kind of connection to the original killers."

"Killer," Ingvild mutters.

"What?"

"Killer. Lucija sure as hell *tried* to kill you and Karla, but she never succeeded. She orchestrated a lot of it, true, but it was LeBeaux doing the killing. Lucija never actually killed anyone."

"*We* did," Karla responds. It shocks me to my core. Why would she even say that?

"Livvy and I both killed, but it doesn't make us killers. Lucija had the *mindset* of a killer though."

"We're straying here." I try to steer back to the goal of the conversation. Karla's comment rocked my flow, and I am not ready to go there. "Suspects. So perhaps the twins have connections to LeBeaux or Lucija. Who else?"

"Erik?" Ingvild asks the group.

"Loser boy who wanted to scare us half a year ago?" Karel

EUROPEA HALLS 2: A SUMMER IN BUDAPEST

lets out a condescending sigh.

"Erik." Time to focus. "Suspect number three. He did send us that text; he even came forward. He might have apologised, but that felt as forced as it gets. He doesn't really know any of us though."

"He was in my Chinese class until he switched, 'cause I basically death stared him each time he walked into the classroom," Karla semi-proudly professes.

Karel agrees with the sentiment. "He went out with Matej and me sometimes, but never in the core circle. More like an acquaintance and even then, we never spoke about anything important. He stopped hanging out with me too after Matej's death."

A dark cloud is blocking the sunshine; it becomes darker in the room. We all instinctively look outside, past the balcony, onto the Danube, its glistening dark grey flow menacingly teasing us, the city looking gloomy and monstrous for a moment. We all feel it. The Chain Bridge has an almost black glow to it now, strengthening the metaphor I've been feeling the last few days. The bridge leading into Pest, into lightness and normality, where the others are. Where people our age who haven't gone through trauma are, ready to pick us up once we cross that bridge, once we walk our way through pain, cleansed by the Danube, onto a new life. There's no bridge left for us.

I shift my head and hone into my slasher knowledge. "Who else?" My gut tightens as I know I am about to head for the hard part. I clench my fists and crack my right thumb. It needs to happen though. "Us four."

The anxiety encircles us, a grey blanket pushing and pulling, testing our friendship.

"Do we really want to go there, Liv?"

"I think we need to, Ing." I lower my head, take a moment, close my eyes and inhale the lavender scent coming from the bathroom. It soothes my racing brain, temporarily at least. "We are all suspects. Ing: when you, Lucija, and I were left standing, we didn't even question each other. Lucija was never even *considered* a suspect. If we want things to go differently this time, we can't make the same mistakes. All of us could be the killer or killers."

I try to find some kind of a hint in all three of my best friends' eyes that they could feel caught, but they all look equally nervous and terrified about how this will evolve.

"Karla, you first."

"Me?" She shudders at the thought of it.

"I want to get you out of the way first, sorry. So Karla. The love interest. Never trust the love interest is one of the rules. Doesn't matter if you're queer. I don't think sexuality has anything to do with this. You're my girlfriend, that makes you a direct suspect. Close to the Final Girl, no one would suspect you, least of all me."

"Can I defend myself or -?" She is shaken.

"Let's not do that. I'm speaking theoretically here, and the more any of us defend ourselves, the more guilty we'll look."

"Damn, this is like a messed-up version of that game Were-wolf where you have to guess who killed the villagers," Karel adds. Not sure why, so I ignore the comment.

"You know me better than most. You were there that night, and you could've faked being scared. So, in sequel world, you are high up on the list." Ingvild's eyes are telling. She's staring at Karla in a suspicious fashion.

"Ing, stop it, don't look at me like that. Livvy, do we really want to do this? We'll all end up being scared of each other when we actually need each other."

"I don't *want* to do this, but you asked me to do this, and I will. Shall we move on?"

"Let's," Karla whispers, seemingly deflated and hurt.

"Karel, the other love interest. Most serial killers are still men. Like, statistically. Also, you're the only one of us who has never been stabbed, let alone stalked by the killer."

Ingvild is most definitely phased by that. "I didn't look at it like—"

"Well, I told you all I was being stalked on this trip. I'm sure of it."

"Stalked is not the same as stabbed, Karel, sorry. You have classic killer profile written all over you. We were never that close before, and for all we know, you could've helped LeBeaux out with the killings. The rest of us were together the whole time. You were never with us during the killings."

"Karla wasn't with us at that time either." Ingvild looks down at the bed sheets.

"Come again?" Karla replies sternly.

"You weren't with us, so what you've said about Karel also applies to Karla." Of course, she wants to defend her boyfriend. I knew this wouldn't be easy.

I take a moment to observe the tension around me. "I don't want this to tear us apart. But we need to be wise and consider all options. That includes me, I know; we can get to me soon. Ing, what you've said about Karla does make sense. Maybe Karla and Karel, K&K, are in this together, and we're oblivious to it all."

Karla is visibly pissed off now. "You really believe any of this?"

"No." That's a lie. I don't know what or who to believe. "At least, I don't want to. But I believed Lucija, blindly. I stepped right into her trap, and she stabbed me."

"Well, then let's move onto your bestie. The BFF." Oh, Karla is mad.

"Fine, Ingvild. The Gale to my Sidney. No one would see that one coming either. Let's be honest, we're sort of the two Final Girls—it's not just me. We both survived the killings."

"Where are you going with this?" Ing scratches her neck, lowering her body even more than she has been.

"People would be shocked if it were you. They'd have sympathy for you for almost dying in the first movie, then being such a good friend to me and—"

"That *better* not be ironic, Liv." Deadpan.

"It's not. You are—you know that. Which is why nobody would suspect you."

I round my lips and exhale a slight gust of air. "I guess that leaves me. Who wants to go for me?" For a moment I suspect them all to grab the chance with both hands to destroy me after everything I've word vommed into the group, but nobody does. "Nobody?"

"I'll go then," Karla whispers. Her face tense and trembling around her upper lip. "The Final Girl. What a twist that'd be. The audience would be mad for sure if Sidney or Laurie or whoever the Final Girl is would end up being the killer. But at least it'd be original. Fresher than the twins."

"How about my motive?"

"You snapped. The PTSD"—she's getting personal, my arms tingle with stress—"had become too much. You couldn't take it anymore. Or some other mental health stuff. Let's face it, you *have* killed someone." This again?

143

Karel is pondering, his eyes upwards, focused on the ceiling and in thoughts. "Or the two of you together. Karla and Oliwia, the power killers. We know you both have it in you."

Karla rebukes: "Or Karel and Ingvild, the two sidekicks, having had enough of not being in the limelight."

That's it, time to call it. This is getting nastier than it ever should've. Not us four. Maybe this was a mistake. Instant guilt crushes my chest. "I think that's enough for now. But let's leave it at this: we do have to be careful, every single one of us. And something else."

They all appear exhausted by my soliloquy. Is it a soliloquy if others chime in too actually? Anyway.

"What is it, Liv?"

"We *cannot* split up. It's the classic slasher trope that ends up getting everyone killed. Alzbeta"—I'm saying their names, not with ease, but this needs to be clear—" was on her own. Ayat walked away from the group. Marieke wasn't exactly alone, but she didn't know Lucija was in on it. What I'm trying to say is, we all need to stick together. All four of us."

"That seems like a bit of a contradiction after having gone through us as suspects?" Ingvild thinks out loud.

"It is, but even then, there's safety in numbers. That means all of us together, at all times. Even for toilet breaks."

"Even for number twos?" Karel breaks the heaviness of this entire conversation and cracks a slight smile. I'm grateful he does.

"For all numbers."

"The death of romance, right there," he adds.

"Better than the death of us," Ingvild defeatedly admits. The room fills with more silence, the tension almost unbearable to hold.

CHAPTER 34

"Well, that was extremely awkward." Karla rubs it in. "So we shouldn't really fully trust each other, but we need to stay together at all times. Fun."

I don't know where to go from here either. These past days had been such a gift to us as a group, getting closer, trying new things, and meeting new people. There was hope. I had hope. Now one text message has taken that away from all of us. I want to go in for a group hug, but I'm not sure who I can trust. I don't want to be that naive again. Lucija has taken that away from me. These walls that had gradually been torn down by the three people around me are now being built back up, higher and thicker than before. That hurts even more than the fear being back. I want to be close to them all, but what if one of them—or more of them—is the killer?

Chapter 35

KARLA

We all stand up and hover around the hotel room aimlessly. I wish this entire conversation had never happened in the first place. It tore a part of our friendship bond, a massive part of our trust. I don't know which one is better: living in denial but being close to each other or being aware that any of us could be lethal. Both options are dangerous. Danger. That word wrecks through my bones. I'm in danger again. We all are.

KOIK. From what I remember about the entire MIOLAA thing, it means either Karel or I is the first to go.

I make a vow to myself, here and now, to trust them. I need to. I can't do this on my own, so I suppose I am going for option one in the end. They can't be killers. I do like the idea of always sticking together, it adds a layer of (false?) protection. I want to tell them all I love them, but I don't know how after the weirdness that has formed between us all. Screw this.

"I love you all." It rolls out, right before the tears do. I don't think I've ever cried in front of Ingvild and Karel, but I couldn't care less right now. They are all startled, not knowing exactly how to reply. Please say it back.

Livvy breaks the moment. "I love you too, boo." She walks over to me and cradles me.

I feel a third hand on my back. "So do I, Karla." It's Ingvild. She joins in on the hug.

"Me too. I love you all." More steadying hands on my back. Karel gives me that warm smile, and there it is; more tears. There's still some uneasy energy between us all, but they probably all need to hold onto us as a group as much as I do. It must be Balazs—I'm almost sure of it now. That dude has the kindest eyes. It's always the kind ones.

My bladder reminds me I can't keep it in forever. I know what that means. "So, if you were serious about us sticking together at all times, this girl needs a potty break."

Ingvild and Livvy smile, but Karel grinds his teeth uneasily. "Maybe just the girls can go together and I—?"

"No!" all three of us shout at the same time.

He lifts up his hands apologetically. "Fine, fine, I'll join, but don't expect me to actually face you as you do your thing. I'll stand in front of the sink, staring at my reflection and wondering how it has all come to this." At least he still sort of has a sense of humor.

Well, that was the most contorted pee of my entire life. They better catch this killer soon or I'll end up with a bladder infection, too scared to pee. I know people won't be too happy about this, but here it goes: "One more thing, I know I'm being a pain right now, but can we get some sodas from that vending machine in the main lobby? That entire conversation, or -well - the stress of it all, has made my mouth so dry."

"Oh, I thought it was just me!" Karel chimes in.

"Same here," Ingvild joins in.

I really need a lemonade and a cigarette, even if Oliwia isn't a fan. She'll get over it.

"Assemble the troupes," Oliwia jokes. The absurdity of us moving everywhere together would be comical if this weren't so creepy at the same time. We all start walking towards the door that leads into the hallway. "After our drink, we need to think of a game plan of how to get the hell out of here unscathed."

I agree, we've been talking about suspects and rules, but we shouldn't just lock ourselves up in our hotel room either.

"I agree, Livvy, we need to figure out what to do. Maybe the cops—"

"No!" Ingvild and Oliwia shout back at me. Ingvild is seething with anger at the thought of it. "No cops. They were of no use to us in Brussels, and I'm not trusting anyone that could have some sort of connection to that detective. Not ever again."

That idea was shut down early. Let's start with sodas then. I reach for the doorknob, the others right behind me, and open the door, walking into the hallway.

I get a message. Just me this time, it seems, as I don't hear the others' phones going off. Unease sets in.

Unknown Number: *KOI*

That mask. The killer, staring deep into my soul. I let out a toe-curdling scream as he stabs me in the stomach with a large kitchen knife. Before I can even turn back to the others, the killer slams the door shut in front of them, still pushing his knife deeper into me, and smashes off the door lock with some metal bar. He's locked them inside the hotel room, leaving me on my own.

My heart sinks. I'm the first 'K' to go. The knife cuts through my intestines, the pain unbearably intense, I hear some horrific sploshing sounds coming from inside me. Dripping noises. *Focus, Karla, don't push things away. Focus.* The others are banging on the door, screaming for help. I can't scream anymore; I'm in too much of a shock. There's no one in the hallway, of course. Typical.

"Run!" That's Oliwia's voice, heavy with despair. She snaps me out of my confusion. Run.

I hit the killer right in his face with a right hook, and as he releases his grip, I push out the knife—the pain will go, the pain will leave—and run to the end of the hallway, down the stairs. He is following me, but I won't give up that easily. I surprise myself at how fast I am after that stab, but there is absolutely no way I am dying. I keep running down the staircase, some woman on one of the landings screaming bloody murder— appropriate? —until I reach the main lobby. My intestines are protesting more with every step. A couple of people are standing in front of the info desk, waiting to be checked in. They all stare at me—or the blood—in disbelief and run outside, not even trying to help me. "Room 426, my friends are locked in!" I manage to hurl at the receptionist as I stumble towards her, my pace now a bit slower. She moves backwards from behind her desk, clutching her heart, as she looks next to me, seeing the killer approaching me. "Miss, run, he's here!" I notice the reflection of the killer in the mirror behind reception. He is inching closer to me from the side. He pulls out the large bloody knife and tries to stab me again, but the weapon cuts deep into the wooden reception desk, right beside me. My heart is pumping in my throat, ready to flee. Screams all around.

"She's bleeding!" One over-intelligent tourist clamours as I run towards the main doors. The dark clouds blur my vision of Buda a bit as I run outside, the figure still an inch behind me.

I hear them. That's Oliwia's voice coming from the balcony. Her wailing is too painful to cope with right now. *Don't look back, Karla.* I don't want to look at her, just in case it's the last time. I can't. Tears well up again, this time a mix of utter fear and fatigue. Keep going. Someone will help.

I run onto the main boulevard leading up to the Chain Bridge with the killer a step behind me. I'm yelling for help to every single person around me. "Help, please, call the cops!" *Sorry Livvy, I need help.* "Help!" There is a mass of people around me as I sprint towards the gigantic lions at the start of the bridge, but nobody seems to understand what is actually happening. Some people look away in disgust; others scream back at me and walk away. Some are recording me with their phones. The crowd of people walking onto the bridge is so thick it slows me down. The killer grabs my hair from behind and stabs me in my upper back. Twice. Or three times, I'm not sure, it's all becoming a mess in my head. The agony is now everywhere, ache flowing through every inch of my body.

I keep moving, now walking rather than running, as there are too many people around me. I'm almost at the middle of the bridge. I feel the figure breathing down my neck, the knife poking in my back. I *cannot* go like this. I let out a frustrating scream as I see more and more people recording me, whispering to the people around them.

An old lady walks up to me and speaks to me in Hungarian, her voice full of distress. She sees the blood and then looks at the killer behind me. She hits him violently with her purse, repeatedly. Pure anger in her eyes. I hear some small grunts and I decide to kick the killer and push through the crowd, making my way forward. I look back to thank the lady, but the figure has turned around and has slit her throat in one grotesque move.

The lady falls onto one of the many onlookers, lifeless, blood pouring from her open gash. More shouting going on around me.

"Move, get out of my way!" I yell exasperatedly as I can tell nobody will help me. A confused middle-aged couple in front of me is taking photos with a selfie stick. I snap it out of the man's arm and smash the stick and phone into the killer's head. More grunting.

I've got him. Keep smashing. I lift and lower the stick, onto his face. There you go, bastard, I'll keep going till you're dead. I'm becoming numb to the swirl of sounds and movement around me in the middle of the bridge.

There's only the killer and me here.

He has tumbled onto the ground in front of me, struck by the stick.

I might have a chance. I scan my body and notice all the blood. I could still make it. No movement on the floor. I think he's actually unconscious.

I did it.

Don't get cocky now, just smash him again. I lift the selfie stick up again ready to hit the final blow, but as I do so, a young boy runs past me in fear and pushes into me, making me fall onto the floor next to the killer. The moment I'm down, he springs up, as if I hadn't even beaten him at all, and throws the phone out of the selfie stick. Then he pushes the bar into my stomach, right into the stab wound as I lay there on the ground, people's feet stomping right next to me.

I howl, I screech—every part of me trying to survive as the

metal stick enters my intestines. This can't kill me though; the stick isn't sharp. *Stay here, don't pass out.* I'm not going to die because of a bloody selfie stick. Hell no.

My back is cracking as I try to stand up, pulling out the stick and throwing it into the Danube next to me. As I twirl the stick away, he grabs me by the shoulders and pushes me towards the edge of the bridge.

Yet more running from bystanders. But no help. Nobody.

I cough up some blood and try to stay present, but I keep falling in and out of consciousness.

I see Livvy's face in front of me. She's kissing me in aisle L of the library, lovers' lane.

Then I wake up again, the edge of the massive bridge, metres above the river. I hear the knife being pulled out and feel it slicing into my lower back. Less controlled, more anger, deeper cuts. The life is being stabbed out of me.

The tears roll down. I know I won't make it. I hope Oliwia will. I hope she'll be safe.

He lifts me, my entire body shaking and failing, over the edge. I see the dark waters glaring at me, waiting for me to swallow me up.

Then he drops me.

Chapter 36

OLIWIA

I had almost jumped off the balcony to run after Karla if it weren't for Karel and Ingvild stopping me. They held me back with all their might as I saw my girlfriend stumbling, running, her body full of blood, a flash of that mask. That horrific, horrid mask I hadn't seen in over a year and a half, except for in my nightmares. I don't know which is worse—seeing her on the street being followed by the killer or not seeing her anymore at all. A million thoughts keep running through my mind. She's resourceful, Karla; she won't go down without a fight. Perhaps she found a way to—

Security breaks down our hotel door, finally. I don't wait for the other two. I sprint. Faster than I ever have. *Come on Karla, fight. I'm coming for you. Hold on.* I cannot have her die on me. A panic button is about to be jammed in my brain, but not now. Now you fight, Liv.

I hear and see a mess of a chaotic crowd with their phones up, coyly walking towards the bridge. Did she run up there? I lost track of where she went after she turned left behind the hotel.

A loud thud pushes my focus. What was that sound? The crowd further down the bridge screams and steps away. I close my eyes for a moment, hoping Karla has thrown the killer off the bridge. *Please* let this be the case. I pick up the pace and run towards the crowd. "Karla? Karla, are you there?"

I look around the group of people, many of them gasping or covering their mouths with their hands. A sense of shock flows through the mass, and I am terrified to find out what has happened. A part of me knows. But it can't be. *Not my girl.*

I pass by the corpse of an old lady whose throat has been slit. Blood-soaked stones and metal underneath. I scream. A macabre hint of relief sets into my stomach. Maybe that's why people are running—the killer hasn't killed Karla. He's killed this poor old lady, but then I glance around the sea of people, almost none of them even realising there's a dead old lady on the ground. There's more to it than that. Exhausted, I pull some teenage boy's arm and ask, "What are you all screaming about?"

His grimace is tense with disgust: "This blonde girl—the ferry."

Blonde. My heart tightens. Girl. No, please not her. My ears start ringing, the top of my fingers tingle and my chest warns me about another attack about to unfold. "What-what do you mean, the ferry?"

He points down further, over the bridge.

I walk, alone—surrounded by these vultures of depravity—to the ledge of the bridge. More hurling sounds are hitting my ears from lower down, by the level of the Danube River.

I stare at my hands, trembling as they hold onto the cold railing of the bridge. If I keep staring at my hands, I won't have to look at the ferry underneath. If I keep staring, she might still be alive. I squint my eyes, glaring at my nail beds, as a blurry red splotch moves underneath me. Red and white. The white ferry. Blood. I can't look. I can't. But I have to, what if it's not her?

I peer down the bridge. There she is. Karla. Her bloodied body crashed onto the deck of the ferry. Her left arm is lying somewhere further down the ferry. Her face almost unrecognisable, her neck twisted in an unnatural position. The people on the boat are still screaming. Why won't they shut up and show some respect for Karla?

She's dead. Karla is gone.

A concoction of anger and heartbreaking pain releases itself, throwing out a wailing cry as I drop to my knees. The tears blur my vision, and I'm glad they do. I can't ever see that again. I won't ever see Karla alive again.

Ping.

Not now, you bastard. I need a moment. I don't want to look at my phone, but the morbid curiosity is too strong.

Unknown Number: *KOI - who's next, Karel or Ingvild?*

Chapter 37

KAREL

Ingvild and I have found her, finally. She's sobbing on the ground in the middle of the bridge. She was too fast; we couldn't keep up. I know what that means. Tears instantly hit my eyes.

Oliwia looks up at us and hurls out: "Karla! She's gone! He took her. She fell onto the ferry. Her arm."

It cuts through flesh and bone, observing that kind of hurt. Seeing your friend absolutely devastated. Ingvild and I go down onto our knees and make a sort of protective shield around Liv, holding her. We all cry into each other's arms. Ingvild squeezes my bicep for comfort. I squeeze back. A little island forms itself around us on the bridge as the onlookers have apparently realised we know the victim. Somehow some insensitive jerks are filming us. I honestly don't have the energy to fight them off. Let them if it adds anything to their pathetic lives. I've lost one of my best friends. Again.

This odd out-of-body sensation takes over. I pan down, seeing the three of us from above, zooming out onto the picturesque yet grotesque city of Budapest. First you feel the hurt and despair of the three people as the lifeless body of their friend is being pulled onto the Pest side. The more you zoom out though, the less it matters. Other sounds and other emotions yell equally loudly, if not more. People are laughing in the parks, walking their dogs, arguing in the kitchen about how to properly do the dishes. That one kill won't change their lives. It'll be a glitch, a moment, when they see it on the news. Some might even pray for her. But most will turn it into a little gossip session about how Budapest has changed. The view zooms out even further, turning the apartments at night into little specks of light. Like this, nobody can sense the pain. Like this, numbness can take over safely.

Buzz.

A rush cuts through my head, zooming me back into the now.

Unknown Number: *Moszar Utca 62. All three of you. Tell anyone else and I'll kill your girl.*

The girls can tell by my body language what has happened.

"What does it say?" Ing wonders.

"We need to go, now."

Chapter 38

OLIWIA

How did this all happen so fast? One minute we were trying to open up again, meeting new people and going out. The next I see Karla, the streaks of red against the sharp white. Karel brought me out of an attack; I was apparently frozen again. My entire body feels weak, as if I'm not entirely here. I don't actually feel pain; I don't feel anything in my body. I don't sense the gravity dragging me down, an all-too-familiar sensation. I'm finding it hard to walk, but Ingvild and Karel are supporting me, carrying me almost, to the address the killer has sent. The breeze is giving me some hints that I'm here, that this is not another nightmare. The mild wind pulls me out of my state of limbo.

My two friends, they still need me. I need them. We can't give up and allow anyone else to die. I knew, deep down, this day would come. I had expected it to happen on the one-year anniversary or when I walked back into Europea for the first time, filled with anxiety and grief. I was sure a killer would pop out of a bathroom stall every time I had to go, so I kept it in until I got back to the dorms. Life there wasn't much better either though. I still walk past the staircase, avoiding the remnants of bloodstains. I haven't gone to any of the EU night parties either. How could I, really? And that library? Forget it—I'm not setting foot in there ever again. A naive part of me hoped a different environment would create a newfound belief that life could be safe, that there were things to be excited about again. The only thing that truly kept me going were the people around me, my relationship with Karla. She did everything for me, and I know she was hurting too. I saw it in those sleepy eyes in the morning. I didn't have the heart to ask if she'd had another bad night, but I knew. I should've checked in on her more, 'cause that's all she ever did. Be there. And now she's not here anymore. I can't make the same mistake with Ingvild or Karel. This isn't about me; it's about us, the trauma we've all gone through.

I remove my arms from their shoulders and try to walk on my own. I'm all right.

"How are you two?" I ask them. They couldn't possibly look more shocked. That says it all right there. I haven't checked in on them enough.

"Coping," Ing replies. "How about you? Can you walk?"

"I can walk. And you, Karel?"

"I'll be fine." We're still not fully honest with each other. Always protecting one another and ourselves against the grief.

"I want to apologise." They both frown.

"Now?"

"Yes, boo, now. I've been so wrapped up in my own thoughts and fears, I haven't been there for you two."

"Are you sure now is the time to—?"

"I'm sure, Karel. We don't know what we're walking into or how long we have left. I should've been there more for you both. I was too caught up with my own emotions and fears. I need to say it now. Look at where we are. No cops, only the three of us. This feels like the library all over again." My mind races. "Which reminds me: we cannot go in unarmed. We need to have some kind of weapon this time."

Adrenaline swiftly removes any anxiety left. This bastard will pay for what he did to Karla. "We need to fight and stick together."

"You're right, Liv. So, what do you suggest we protect ourselves with?"

Chapter 39

BALAZS

I am glad Szofi's driving. I wouldn't be able to focus right now, and somehow, with her gaze being this fixed on the road, I know she'll get us out of Budapest safely. It doesn't sit well with me though, leaving people behind that obviously need help. Not too sure what it is I could help with, but running away isn't it.

"Sis, are you okay?"

"Let me drive, bro. I love you, but let me drive. I can't focus if I have to think." She sounds stern, but there are pools of tears welling up. I know her. Let her be for a bit. Looking at my sister, maybe this was the right move in the end. I can't even *think* about anything happening to her. She's always been my rock, and I hope I have been hers too. We haven't known these people for long, so why would we jeopardise our lives for some summer friends?

Oliwia's breakdown was hard to watch though. Seeing someone so fragile and in a state of panic, I wish I could've done more. If I hadn't brought up the Szechenyi party, Andreea and Mihails would have still been alive. That thought keeps creeping through my mind, tugging at my heart strings. Am I to blame?

I get a text message.

Szofi is instantly rattled, but firmly reorganises her thoughts and focuses on the road again. I try to hide my panic; it's a good thing she is looking ahead rather than at me.

"Sis, you should park for a moment." My tone stays as calm as possible, given the circumstances. I need to keep her safe.

She knows all too well that I mean business. She takes a turn and drives down a desolate side street where she parks. She is still looking ahead, too afraid to make eye contact. Too afraid of the text.

"Well? What does it say?"

I gather up the courage, as if plowing through quicksand. I'm not sure how I can do this.

"Tell me. Please." She sounds a tad bit more unnerved now. She deserves to know.

"It's an attachment. A photo."

For the first time in what feels like ages, she looks me in the eyes. "A photo? Show me."

A part of me was almost happy to bear the burden of knowing what is in that photo. Now she is in on it too.

The photo shows our mom and aunt, sitting together outside on my aunt's porch. They are all smiles and chatting away, by the looks of it.

"Who sent this?" Her throat sounds hoarse, the full-fledged panic kicking in hard.

"It's an unknown number."

"Well, is there a way to trace the number? It must be the same person that sent, you know."

We sit there in silence for a couple of seconds. I know how she thinks; she knows how I think. It's the killer. There's no other explanation.

Another text.

We both jump up, Szofi hitting the horn of the steering wheel with her fist, leading us to jolt even more.

Unknown Number: *Moszar Utca 62, come now. Both of you. No cops or mommy and aunty die.*

Chapter 40

INGVILD

The past hour has been an absolute whirlwind. It appears as though we were coasting through life the past three days, finally almost enjoying it, before Karla's death snapped us back into our reality. Our reality doesn't have space for parties or spa days; ours is only about survival.

It wasn't much of a walk here; I suppose that was the plan all along. From the Chain Bridge to wherever it is they are leading us to, we all walk with Swiss Army knives in our right hands, which we have picked up from a night shop on our way. There's no way we are going in unarmed like last time. Not exactly a Michael Myers knife, but it'll do on such short notice.

As we walk up to the dark street of Moszar Utca, the sun setting at the exact right—or wrong—time, the towering derelict building ahead shows us where to go. Number 62. Karel, Oliwia, and I exchange knowing looks.

"Act Three," Liv mutters.

"Say what?" Karel asks, genuinely interested.

"Never mind."

The smell of rotten meat and old furniture hits our nostrils as we enter through the main door. It's almost pitch black in here, so we have all turned on the torchlight of our mobiles. Dust particles float through the vast room, accentuated by our artificial lights. This building has not been in use for a while, that's for sure. I observe the geometric Soviet style shapes around me, this is as Brutalist as it comes. On a normal day, I would've loved to explore this beast of a building—Urbex much? —but now, all I feel is dread. Well, not only dread but also a bit of escapism, observing the architecture around me rather than looking for a killer. I turn my phone to the ceiling, illuminating old rusty meat hooks that hang ominously through the silence. A slight rustle of the chains shows that the old windows no longer serve their purpose. A white-blueish beam from outside hits the hooks, making them look even more ungodly.

We were all brought here for a reason, but I'm not sure any of us wants to find out what that is. Nothing good can come of being in an abandoned building in a quiet part of the city.

I turn to Liv. "Game plan?"

The tears have dried up and have been swapped with a determined, razor-sharp frown. "This is their lair. This is where we find out more about why Karla—" She can't finish the sentence. Not yet. It takes time; I know that much by now.

"But what do we do? Just sit and wait?"

"We stick to the original plan. No splitting up at any time. Ever."

Karel clenches his fists. "Somehow, I have become a bigger fan of that plan than initially. What *is* this place?"

Liv waves off his comment. "Some sort of an old meat factory —I don't know. Anyway, we need to walk around back against back, so we can spot the killer from different angles. Make sure our backs are never exposed."

I nod in agreement, so does Karel. He still isn't too happy with Oliwia's lack of—which I am painfully aware of right now—plan though. "But what do we actually do now?"

"We wait. I'm sure the killer or killers know we are here. The plan has been set into motion. Do you all have your knife in hand?"

We both nod again.

"Great. It's time."

Chapter 41

OLIWIA

"Hello, everyone."

We all jump up and shine our torches towards the entrance. It's the twins. Karel can barely see them, as our formation with three backs against each other means he is turned the other way.

"I knew it was them!" Ingvild exclaims.

Balazs and Szofi's faces look angular, the light hitting them from underneath. Their long black curls like Medusa's locks, softening the harsh features. I wait for them to speak. It's never this easy.

Balazs steps forward. "No, it's not us! I received a text from an—"

"Unknown number?" Karel asks, obviously suspicious of what's to come.

"Exactly. They gave us this address. No cops allowed or our mom and aunt would die."

Ingvild, Karel, and I look at each other, unsure of what to do next.

"Show us the text," Ing commands, as if a text couldn't be faked. But then again, better than nothing at this point. "Don't walk too fast, show us from a distance." We all pull up our lame excuse for knives a bit higher.

The twins meekly walk towards us, Balazs showing the text. Why are they here? They're not even part of the acronym. Collateral, perhaps?

Szofi steps a bit closer. "We genuinely don't know why we are here either. I imagine this looks sus as hell, but I swear on my brother's life."

Balazs continues, "I swear on my sister's. And on our dog Blanche."

Szofi throws a confused glance at her brother, going "Why?" when he added the family's pet. They both look at the three of us, confused.

"Wait." Balazs says. "How about Karla? Where is she?"

A deep cut. I glance at Ing, hoping she can utter the words that are too painful for me right now. She gets it, she always does.

"She's dead. The killer got her." The twins look shocked, I notice tears in Balazs's eyes. Ingvild picks up on their body language. "We'll explain everything later, but for now we have to stick together and kill whoever did this to her."

Everyone stands around awkwardly, not too sure about what's next. Something needs to happen here, so I take charge. "Right, we're all here now. Whatever it is that is about to commence, it can start." We all nervously wait for an answer from the masked killer somewhere in the dark crevices of the building. "We're here, did you hear me? What do you want from us?" I shout, not entirely convinced that was a great call. Ingvild neither, from the looks of it. The echoes of my terrified voice bounce off the walls, flowing further into the darkness of the factory. This would be a good place to harmonise. Karel better not start singing Chandelier again like he does in every church we've visited. *Focus, Liv.*

The lights switch on. All of us scream and hold onto each other. A row of what looks like cold blue hospital lights hover above us, showing exactly how deep this room is. I hurriedly scan the room, but there's nothing special here. Just a bunch of meat hooks and old desks with some paperwork on it. Hold on. Those folders. Why would there be folders here?

"What are those?" Szofi nods towards the files on the desk to our right.

"No idea. I didn't spot them in the dark," I reply. We all walk to the desks, holding hands and arms like a sick version of Twister. I unhook my arm from Ingvild's and take a dark orange folder. There's no dust on them. This has been recently planted here.

"What does it say?" Karel peers over the heads of the girls, his height nearly rivaling Balazs's.

I take a moment. Whatever was put here is undoubtedly crucial information.

"Open it!" Balazs almost shouts. I do.

I scratch my head. It doesn't make any sense. It's some sort of legal paperwork in Hungarian.

"Well?" Balazs continues.

"Well, I don't know. I think it's in Hungarian. Can you two come over and have a look?"

The twins eagerly shuffle to me, Szofi grabbing the folder from my hands. The tension in the eerily-lit room rises. What the heck is this?

"It's a birth certificate," Balazs almost whispers.

"A what? Whose is it?" Ingvild ponders.

169

Karel screams a sharp cry. We all turn around in a flash and see Karel being dragged down to another room by the killer, Karel's face in sheer terror.

"Karel!" Ingvild cries out.

The killer throws open a door on the far left and pulls Karel into it.

We all run towards the door, but as we do, the lights are turned off again. We are being played with. Toyed with. I continue hopping towards the door, turning my torchlight on again. "This way; they went in there!" We all move to the back end of the room, but when I try to turn the doorknob, it's locked. Of course.

"Open it, Liv!" Ingvild cries out.

"I can't; it's locked!"

"Well, force it then! Balazs?"

The tallest of the group runs to the door and starts banging it, when suddenly four cold lights turn on to our right.

It's Karel and the killer.

He is dragged into what looks like an old office, with large glass windows everywhere instead of walls.

"Karel!" Ing yells again, seeing Karel being held hostage, his mouth covered by a gloved hand. The killer shows us all the machete he is holding, lifting it up and moving it from left to right, taunting us. Karel is too scared to move.

Ingvild sprints to the windows a second faster than the rest of us, trying to break it. We all join in, shouting and banging like a bunch of mad maniacs.

"It won't budge! What kind of glass is this?" Ing asks herself out loud.

She places her hands onto the glass. "Don't you dare hurt Karel!" The veins in her temple pulsate. She is filled with rage.

"I'll kill you!"

Chapter 42

INGVILD

I know my guy. He is trying not to show how scared he is, but his eyes speak volumes. We are all banging on the windows to no avail.

"Our knives!" I yell out. I pull out the Swiss Army knife and stab the window repeatedly, leaving only a hint of a crack here and there.

Balazs steps back. "This won't work. It's bullet proof glass or something like that."

"In an old shop like this?" Szofi wonders.

"Well, it's not normal glass, is it?"

I want to smack them both in the face. "Keep trying, are you kidding me? Come on!" Oliwia looks at me in panic. She knows Karel means the world to me; I can't lose him. A shot of realisation sets in. This is how Liv felt before she found Karla dead. It's the worst impending doom I've ever felt in my life.

No, not to Karel.

There must be something else we can do. He's helped me all these months with my recovery, it's time for me to help him. But how?

The lights in the office room switch off. We all scream. I feel sick to my stomach, cold sweat budding on my forehead.

"Karel! Karel, are you okay? Balazs, keep trying the door. We'll try the windows!"

He nods and frantically elbows the door, stepping back a bit further each time to obtain more of an impact.

The lights flash back on, blinding us all for a short moment. Then I see them, the stab wounds on his arms, the glistening blood trickling down. His face is no longer being held by the figure's hand. He's screaming out for us, for help, but we can't hear him. Only barely, actually. Soundproof room. What *is* this place? His hands are banging onto the windows too, but not as hard as ours, as he looks like he's in a lot of pain. My man, don't give up.

"Karel!" I don't know what else to say or do, so I stab a milimetre deeper into the unbreakable glass with my ridiculously tiny knife. He's still alive, it's just his arms. He can make it out alive. I was stabbed everywhere, and I made it; so can he.

Lights off, again. That bastard is messing with us all.

"Come on, Balazs, please!" I cry out of frustration that Szofi, Liv, and I aren't getting any closer to breaking the glass. We're all exhausted, but the adrenaline keeps us going.

Lights on. No, no, no. I cry out his name as I see the machete being pulled out of his stomach, blood spewing out the gaping hole. Karel is holding onto his intestines, confused and far too pale-skinned. He gazes into my eyes and mouths, "I love you. I'm sorry." I say it back to him, the tears flooding down.

"Ingvild, Oliwia, maybe this is our chance?" Szofi wonders.

"To what?" Liv sharply asks.

"To escape. I know that sounds horrible, but if you think rationally—"

"There *is* no rational thinking involved here. He's our best friend," she hisses back at Szofi. "So either keep banging this

173

window or get the hell out of here, 'cause Ing and I aren't going anywhere." Liv nods at me. She's in this with me until the end.

Thank you, boo.

The twins hesitate for a moment, but, to my surprise, continue the incessant stomping.

"Thank you," I whisper through my tears. I move my view back to my boyfriend.

Lights out.

"I can't anymore, Liv, I can't. This is too much." I fall into her arms and almost slide down to my knees, but she makes sure I stand up.

"I understand. Trust me, I do, but do not give up. Ever." She holds onto my wrists and places them back to the glass. "Just try, or you'll hate yourself for the rest of your life."

So I try. Stabbing away at little chips of glass. I know it's pointless. I hear a very faint cry for help. Please don't die on me, Karel. I need you. I can't do this without you.

The lights go back on. It's just Karel this time. His eyes find Oliwia's, then mine, and he has a very gentle, peaceful smile on his face. His entire face starts bleeding in the middle, from the top of his crown down to his chin. He's been cut in half.

Balazs and Szofi scream, Szofi vomiting her soul out onto the floor. Liv and I have seen these horrors before. It's never been him though. I never thought he wouldn't make it. His eyes start trembling before he flops down lifeless onto the floor. The moment he does, Balazs cracks open the door and face-plants into the office. The worst of timings possible. We all jolt into the room. I need to hold my boyfriend.

The lights go off again. I search for my phone so I can turn the torchlight on and kiss Karel one last time. Then I hear it, the faintest of pressured air sounds. I swipe onto my main screen and switch on the torch. White-greyish gas is coming from all sides of the office.

"It's gas!" Liv screams, "Get out!"

But before we can even move, the world in front of me goes pitch black.

Chapter 43

SZOFI

Images of Balazs, the group, and me race through my mind. Us dancing at Instant and Szechenyi, my brother effortlessy sliding from group to group like the social butterfly he is. I've always been a bit envious of that, but at the same time, his extrovert self has dragged me out of my shell multiple times. Thanks to him, I've met so many people I wouldn't have gotten to know on my own. If it were up to me, I'd be in my sofa listening to true crime podcasts and reading thrillers all day long. It hasn't necessarily been easy, being the twin to Mister Social. There have been times I felt like Balazs's shadow, but he has this way of making me feel equally important that I almost believe it myself. Almost. People kind of just expect us to be the same, just 'cause we're twins. We're not though, not at all, but the symbiosis works for us. The flashes I have of his smile turn into a saddened grimace. The whirlwind of the past couple of days comes rolling down on me, thrusting me back into the here and now.

My entire body aches, constricted and tied up in this chair. My wrists have been pulled together behind my back by horrifically sharp barbed wire. In a way, it's a relief I can't see my arms. I know it doesn't look pretty. It sure doesn't feel pretty. A part of me knew we'd end up in danger when I met those people from Brussels. Something about that entire group felt off from the get-go. I have no idea who to trust except for Balazs. I've listened to one too many podcasts to know I'm in the hot seat right now, quite literally. It's my turn to face the killer.

Chapter 44

INGVILD

The muffled sound ringing in my ears becomes sharper until I realise it's my own incessant coughing. Far too bright hospital-like lights hit my eyes, an instant jab onto my skull. Where am I?

I spring up, searching for the others. I'm alone in here. It appears I am still in the same building; the same architectural style and bile-inducing smell orientate me back. It's not the same room though. This is a small room with nothing around me except for an old black chair and desk on the right side. I'm probably locked in, but it never hurts to—oh wait. The door's not locked.

I push down the doorknob and carefully open it. This is too easy. I need to stay alert here. The killer has obviously planned something. What were the twins about to say about that birth certificate anyway. Whose was it? I need to find Karel. Karel. My stomach tightens, ripping inside. He's not here anymore. Oliwia and I have both lost our partners. It's just her and me now. She's still out there, the only one left from Europea Halls beside me. Our group halved in a matter of hours. I don't have the time to even try to fathom that. I need to make sure no one else goes. The pain that sets in is too much to cope with for now. My entire chest closes up, wrapping up the grief tightly so it won't escape. Hold onto this feeling; you need it to survive. I nod to myself; you need to make it through. For Liv. And myself—I owe it to myself.

This entire place is a massive playground for the killer. He was surely enjoying my tears, switching those lights on and off like a little showcase of his talents. That twisted maniac. I'm not sure I can trust those two Hungarians, but I'd give my life for Liv. I know she would too.

I step outside the room, my nose and mouth still getting over the chemicals I inhaled. It's a long hallway. God, I hate long hallways. And staircases. Not now. This doesn't have to be the same again. I'm not in the boarding school. A part of me wants to cry out for the others, but that's probably a dumb idea. I could text Liv, but what if her sound is on and the killer hears it? I was brought to this location for a reason, but I hate that this is not my home turf. I have no idea where to start. I don't even know which floor I'm on. I open the door to my right as quietly as possible and step inside. It's almost identical to the one I woke up in. I walk towards the small, dirty windows and see the minuscule streetlights outside. I'm high up. Great, stairs. Again.

I walk down the corridor until, to my surprise, I notice a lift. I think Liv calls it an elevator, anyway. Slim chance it still works, but worth a try. I click on the button on the left side. Rustling noise and metallic clinking, it does—it actually works. Does that mean people are still living or working here? That can't be; it looks like it's been deserted since the fall of the Wall. Or earlier even. Perhaps this is a hideout, some underbelly of Budapest that uses this place for grim purposes.

Pling. The rusty lift doors move, I take one step back and try to grab my pocketknife, but it's not there anymore. Of course. They took it from me.

The doors open. I inhale briskly. Nobody is inside. Okay, get in, go one floor down and look for the others. Which floor is this one? What am I even doing? I click on the up button, but it doesn't work. Okay, that means I'm on the sixth floor. I press "five" and then down. The brain fog is stopping me from thinking clearly. I didn't even check all the rooms on this floor, but I guess I would've heard them if they were here.

The doors open. I walk out onto an exact copy of the other corridor. It's darker in here. I don't see any rooms lit up. I don't want to take any chances though, so I shuffle down the hall and look left and right into all the different rooms. A metallic smell rushes past me. I'm not sure what that means. No sound to be heard anywhere though, except for my stifled breathing. I don't think anyone's here, but I need to be sure.

I open all the doors on the fifth floor, but nobody. I still don't feel too well, so the idea of perusing through four more floors of warehouse rooms mentally exhausts me a bit, but this is Oliwia we're talking about here. I'd rummage through the entire city for her. No other choice then, so I make my way back to the lift. It's still there, waiting for me to continue on in this morbid quest.

I click on "four" and press down again. Stay alert, you never know where the killer is hiding.

The doors open. Nobody. No lights anywhere either on this floor. I still walk out, going through the same routine as on the previous floor.

A loud thud from the back of the hallway. No, not exactly there. I think it's—another thud. Screaming. Multiple voices. My heart races, drumming into my throat. That's them—

they're in danger. I run to the end of the corridor, following the voices. They're on the third floor. *You know what you have to do.*

I take a single moment to breathe in more deeply and lower my shoulders before I step back towards the lift. I can't tell what my game plan is yet, but they need help.

I click on "three" and press down. This is it. Whatever is waiting behind these lift doors, I'm about to find out. I sway my body back and forth in an attempt to convince myself I've got this. The door opens.

That mask.

The killer pushes me against the back of the lift and closes the door behind him. Now it's time to scream. "Liv, I'm here! In the lift—help me!" He is opposite me, no escape. He pulls out the blood-soaked machete and swings it towards my left hand. Into my scar, blood dripping down onto the lift panel. The pain, a reminder of what I've been through before. The cut isn't that deep, but this can't be a coincidence. It's like a jab at last time. I want to ask how he knows about my scar, but I refrain and try to push him off me. The figure doesn't budge though. Deep pools of vacant eyes stare at me as he swooshes down the machete into my shoulder. It hacks deep into the flesh, the agony making me want to vomit. I am off-balance and about to fall down, but he lifts me up with a sole hand, my entire body pushed up high against the back of the lift, floating off the ground. He's ready to stab me again. The black spots limiting my vision are all too familiar. I squint my eyes and peer at the buttons of the lift, the door must open up again sooner or later. He's pressed "zero". We're on the second floor now. Hang in there, make a run for it once the doors open. He lowers the machete and cuts deep into my stomach. The light pink flesh of my intestines makes its way out of my body as I desperately try to push it back in. There's blood everywhere. *Stay here, don't lose consciousness.* I can bite through the stabs; I've done it before. I'm still lifted up, my feet dangling into nothingness. "Liv, help please! Liv!" I want to shout Karel's name, but a painful reminder stops me. What if I don't make it out alive this time? After everything I've been through?

What can I do to make it out– play dead. Might as well try. I close my eyes and lower my head, exhaling an exaggerated sigh. The doors of the lift open. He releases his hold, and I flop down onto the ground. Every single inch of my body hurts, but I still keep my eyes closed. Play dead. It could work. The doors of the lift close again. He's gone. He actually left. Is he playing with me, or does he really think I'm gone? I want to spring up, but my body is not allowing any sudden movements, so I meekly crawl instead, pressing "three."

I've made it. I'm coming, Liv.

Chapter 45

SZOFI

I jolt up. There he is—the killer. I try to untie my hands, but they're stuck in the barbed wire. I forcefully spring up and down in the chair; I will *not* let this to be the end of me.

"Balazs, Oliwia, wake up! He's here!"

They're responding, confused gazes full of agony.

"Bro, run! Get out!" But then I notice it. It was too hard to spot at first in the dark. They're both chained onto the wall with their hands. Panic overpowers me; we're all stuck here.

Balazs comes to and yells at the killer: "Don't you dare put a hand on my sister!" Oliwia frowns her eyebrows, which makes him add "—or Oliwia. Leave us alone. What do you want from us, anyway? What did we ever do wrong?"

The killer slides past me, a cold breeze hitting my back. I tense up even more. He walks to the end of the room—it's about the size of a classroom—and clicks the "on" button of the TV. He's really messing with us now.

Chapter 46

OLIWIA

I hear Szofi's screams as if they came from the other side of a tunnel. As the echoes hit my forehead, I open my eyes. Everything is sore, I need to—my hands. I look down at the heavy chains around my wrists. There's blood trickling down to the ground, at least I think there is. It's quite dark in here. Who else is in here? Where is Ing? I notice Balazs next to me, stuck in the same position. He is yelling at his sister, who is tied up on a chair, facing us, and—

There he is. The killer is standing next to a large TV screen, tilting his head and making sure we are all conscious again. He is holding the bloody machete in his left hand. I have no clue what I'm about to see, but perhaps it's linked to that birth certificate. I want to ask the Hungarians what they saw, but I'm afraid if I do so in front of the killer, they might end up dead. The worst part is that Ingvild isn't here. What if this is all a big setup and the twins are working together with the killer? I've been here before.

Don't make the same mistake again. Keep your guard up.

My fingers are turning numb, but I'm not sure if it's because of the chains or my PTSD. Whichever it is, I can't let it control me, not now.

The TV turns on, and all we see is a black screen. I try to decipher the looks on the twins' faces, but they appear just as terrified as I am.

"Bro, stay quiet. I'm okay, I'm fine." Szofi is trying to calm down Balazs, who has kept on yelling this entire time. The noise makes me dizzy.

He turns to me: "Are you okay too, Oliwia?"

"I'm okay, as far as that's possible. Have you two seen Ingvild?"

They both say, "No." My deepest, darkest fear: losing Ingvild. Please, no. She must be around here somewhere. She's a fighter; she wouldn't just give up.

The killer puts down his machete and starts typing something on a keyboard that I hadn't noticed before, leaning on an old grey desk. He's got our attention. All the chaos has turned into laser focus.

"TONIGHT, SZOFI, YOU MUST CHOOSE" pops up on the TV in large neon green letters. I'm a little disappointed the killer isn't using a voice changer—vocoder, is it? —but then it hits me: I'm not in some B-movie. I suppose the acronym text game has evolved.

Szofi stares at the screen, looking over her left shoulder as the TV and killer are behind her. Sweat is building on her forehead.

"Choose what?" she whispers.

The figure continues typing. The seconds feel like eternity. My face is glued to the screen, waiting. I feel so helpless, tied up, not knowing where my best friend is. I am trying to come up with a plan, but I can't string thoughts together properly as the TV shows another message.

"BALAZS OR OLIWIA. ONE MUST DIE. CHOOSE NOW."

Chapter 47

BALAZS

My sister is shouting and contorting her body on the heavy chair, desperately trying to claw her way out of the situation.

"I won't! I won't choose!" she keeps yelling, tears streaming down her face. She keeps throwing me apologetic looks, as if it's *her* fault she's in this position.

Oliwia is shockingly calm. She nods at both Szofi and me, implying she knows who Szofi'd choose. One lonely tear runs down her right cheek. "It's okay," she semi-whispers to me. "I get it."

Szofi, on the other hand, is still in a fit of utter rage, refusing to comply with the killer's demand. I wish I could calm her down like I usually do, but I'm not exactly my usual self either. Oliwia or me. One of us could be killed any second now. The strain in my hands gives me that extra push to stay present.

The figure is typing again, seemingly emotionless. "NOW."

Her screams are over. She looks completely deflated, sobbing away, her head lowered into a defeated position. If she's not even making eye contact with me, would she be capable of saving Oliwia instead? What is going through her mind? I know my sister, but we've never been in a situation like this before. What if I'm the one to go?

"I can't choose someone. I won't. Nobody is going to die here because of me." Her voice sounds steadier now. She lifts up her chin and stares into both of our eyes. "They're both good people; I won't."

Terror bolts through me when I realise the killer could end up killing Szofi instead if she doesn't choose.

"Sis, pick me. Please, just do it. He might kill you instead if you don't choose."

Her eyes shoot up with even more tears. "How could you even ask that of me? I couldn't ever choose you over me."

"Choose me then," Oliwia interjects. I glance at her, and I can tell she means it. "Of course you would never pick your brother. You two have been nothing but kind to me. It's okay. Just do it."

Szofi stammers for a moment. "I-I don't know. I can't sentence you to death like that, Oliwia. You've been through so much!"

"Do it, Szofi, it's me or your brother. We all know the answer. Say my name."

The killer stands behind Szofi, not moving much, waiting on a reply, but it seems like he's got all the time in the world. This sicko is probably enjoying it.

I want to tell my sister to pick me instead, but I know she wouldn't do that; so I remain quiet, as bad of a person as that makes me feel. Oliwia could be killed because of my silence. How could I ever live with that though?

"Choose me!" Oliwia yells now, more tears. "You don't have time!"

Szofi lets out an alienesque growl of pure and utter frustration. "Fine! Fine, damn it, I choose Oliwia!"

187

We all resort back to silence in a heartbeat, looking up at the killer. He walks back to the keyboard.

The three of us look at each other. Szofi whispers, "I'm sorry" to Oliwia.

She replies with an "I understand" that is barely audible. Then Szofi turns to me and gives me a faint smile. "I had to, bro."

The screen changes up again. "WRONG CHOICE."

"What? But you told me I had to—? I don't get it." Szofi switches back to frantic mode.

That one move made me understand what's about to unfold in front of my eyes—the moment he grabbed the machete. He steps towards my sister, facing her back. It's her. Szofi is the next to go. I can't watch this.

"Please, no, no. I didn't understand what I was supposed to do. Ask me again. I swear." He lowers his posture and puts his head on her left shoulder in an antagonising manner.

"Get off me, you freak—don't touch me!"

That lights a fire from deep within me. "Don't touch my sister! Kill me instead, don't hurt her!" Both of us are yelling now, a sea of sound praying for the tide to turn. But it doesn't.

He lifts his machete and flings it in her neck. The sound bites through my whole being. I won't look, I can't. For the first time in what feels like forever, I hear Oliwia screaming.

Szofi is still crying; she's still alive. I look back up and see the killer pulling the machete out of her neck, blood dripping out of her from behind.

He hacks into her neck a second time. Szofi tilts her chin upwards and yells whilst staring at the ceiling. She doesn't want to look into my eyes. He doesn't pull the machete out this time.

Oliwia murmurs, "I'm so sorry, Balazs." I don't know how to reply. That's my sister right there.

The killer starts using the machete as a saw and cuts from left to right through her neck. Slow at first, then picking up the pace. She starts making gurgling noises, the machete now almost reaching her throat. A mechanic whizzing cuts through torn flesh. All the yelling and grotesque sounds flow into one. I can't look away this time because I want to be there for her in her last moments. Even if that means looking into her eyes without being able to do anything else. The anger is revolting in my body, as I am left powerless and defenseless because of those chains. All the yanking and pulling doesn't help.

"Look at me, sis." She stares at me with hazy eyes, her entire clammy face pale as the moon. "I love you."

"I love—" She tries to speak, but blood spurts out of her mouth and neck instead.

The killer cuts the last strings of her neck until my sister's head falls down into her own lap. I want to shout, to cry, to kill, everything at once, but I can't. I feel paralysed.

I wish I were dead instead.

Chapter 48

OLIWIA

I try to bring him back, but Balazs is completely out of it. His eyes are wide open, staring in the direction of Szofi's headless body. The triggers are all there, but somehow, I manage to push back an attack. No flight possible with these chains, but no fight either.

The killer puts his machete down again onto the wall and makes his way over to the keyboard. He isn't done just yet.

"NOW FOR THE TWIST."

That brings Balazs back, even though he still appears extremely fragile.

Is Balazs the twist? That folder in the main lobby, perhaps? I glare at the screen, waiting on an update.

A loud thud, blood. A metallic clattering. What has happened? The killer has been hit by something. Something hard by the looks of it, blood trickling over the white mask.

He droops down, machete still in hand. I see what looks like a metal pole. It's Ingvild.

"Ing! You're alive!" I shout through more tears. No idea how one human can produce this many tears in one night, but they keep on coming. Ingvild locks eyes with me and pulls a wide smile.

"Barely," she replies. Only now do I notice all the stab wounds.

The killer is still lying on the ground, motionless.

"Oh damn, are you okay, boo?"

"I will be." I can tell by the brief replies that she doesn't have much strength left. The joy is quickly overtaken with worry.

She walks over to us and stops for a second when she sees Szofi's corpse.

"Balazs." She turns to him. "I'm so sorry."

He nods at her. "We've all lost people tonight, haven't we?"

That one hits home. Karla, Karel, and now Szofi. None of us will walk out of here unscathed.

"Move your head away" she says to me before she smashes the metal pole onto the chains several times. It takes longer than she'd like. "I'm sorry. I'm feeling a bit weak," she mumbles.

With one more swing of the pole, she breaks my chains. I run for her arms and hug her. She winces. "Not too hard, Liv, I'm hurting." I can feel the strength in her body evaporating as her knees start trembling. She loses consciousness.

"Oliwia, my turn!" Balazs pleads. "Free me, please, then we can help Ingvild!"

Both the killer and Ingvild are now on the floor. The figure is positioned far enough for us to run past once I break Balazs' chains. Should I though? How do I know if I can really trust him?

"Please." He looks deep into my eyes. God Liv, his sister has been killed, of course it's not him. Unless that's the twist.

I think he can sense my doubt. "It's not me, I swear. I-I want to get out of here. Give my sister-"—this time it is his turn to break down—"- a proper burial."

191

There's no way he could be this good an actor, so I smash the pole into the chains until he is freed. He gives me a grateful look.

"Help me with Ing. We need to get her to the hospital." Balazs and I pull Ingvild up by the shoulders and carry her, he and I forming a bridge to support her.

We wobble past the killer as Ingvild regains consciousness. "Wait," she notes: "Don't we want to know who's underneath that mask?"

Chapter 49

INGVILD

"You're right," Liv replies. It's time to know who's behind all of this.

"Hold onto Ingvild, will you?" she asks Balazs as she pushes my arm over his tall shoulders. He looks at me with the kindest yet saddest eyes.

"At least I can still help you," he mumbles at me. The poor guy—I can't imagine what it must've been like for him to see his sister die. But then again, I saw Karel die, so perhaps I do know a thing or two about what he is going through. Still, they were twins; that's a whole other level of grief.

Oliwia lowers her body, holding the metal pole in her right hand and reaches out her left to pull off the mask. "Ready?" she whispers at us without looking back. I guess she knows you should never turn your back towards the killer. Good girl. My slasher connoisseur is back.

For a second, the world stops. Freeze frame. Who will it be this time around? Who's even left alive?

"Ready," Balazs and I reply in unison. I'm so ready for this night to be over.

Liv hunches down a bit further and turns her hand into a claw- like shape, about to snatch the bloodied mask from the killer's face.

The figure jumps up and pulls Oliwia's hair, pushing her face towards his.

"Liv!" I scream, not sure what else to do, feeling fainter by the minute. Luckily, she came prepared. She instantly smashes the killer's face with the metal stick until he releases his grip. More blood is spouting from the killer's head, but it doesn't seem to slow him down much.

He stands up tall and proud, taking a big inhale and gaining energy from looking at our fear-filled eyes. We all scream. That reminds me of what Liv had mentioned about Lucija. She said at one point during their final showdown, she looked almost demon-like, a supernatural strength in her bones. Maybe it's the rush from killing, knowing you are on a mission. Whatever it is, that's exactly what it feels like, observing this towering demon. "Run!" Oliwia shouts, hooking her arm around my shoulder so the three of us jolt out of the room, clasping onto each other. She is still carrying the metal stick, the only defense we have with us. We run through the doorframe and back into that drearily long hallway. At least it's lit up this time, as I can see the massive concrete slabs of Brutalist angst around me. I spot the lift at the end of the corridor and spot the streaks of blood splattered all over it. My blood.

"There's an elevator here?" Oliwia sounds surprised.

"Yes, that's how I found you all. I was on a different floor. " I run out of breath.

"Save your strength, keep running!" Balazs adds.

The figure storms out past the doorframe, following us. I look back to see how far away he is from us, and the answer is not nearly damn far enough. They're practically dragging me across the floor now, as I don't have the power to walk anymore.

The stab wounds are pulling stronger and stronger. There's not much time left for me.

"I'm slowing you down, leave me." I wince. I won't have them get killed because of me.

Oliwia takes one single glance at me and unhooks her arm. Wait, is she actually leaving me? There's something odd in her eyes, something I have never quite seen before.

Chapter 50

OLIWIA

That one sentence was all I needed to hear. She needs me. Enough running. Look where that has gotten us. I crack my knuckles around the metal bar, holding onto it with both hands, and walk towards the killer.

"Liv, no, what are you doing?" Ingvild shrieks.

"I'm done running! Balazs, take Ingvild outside."

"Liv, no, I'm not leaving—"

"*Now!*" I yell as I inch closer to the figure, a mere couple of steps away.

Ingvild's baffled expression distracts me for a second, but I can't lose her too. Balazs obliges and runs outside towards the main hall with Ingvild. I hope they'll be fine. I can't think about that right now.

The machete is at the same height as my makeshift weapon. On the same side as well. The figure and I are mirroring each other. I have no fear this time around. Only anger.

"Did you really think I'd keep running?"

The killer tilts his head again, an odd reminder of Europea Halls. This psycho has the exact same body posture and height.

Something about that unnerves me. Who else was there that night?

"Were you there? In the halls? Have you been behind this entire thing?" I want answers, and somehow, I naively hope the killer will answer. You never know, he could need a little push, and I might pull a sensitive string.

"Did LeBeaux boss you around? There's no way you came up with all of this on your own, right?" Talking directly to the person who has murdered my girlfriend ignites my rage to the next level.

A small flicker of light pierces through my eyes as the hallway lights are reflected in the machete. A tiny flinch, but I noticed it—he's moved the machete. An emotional response. I am getting somewhere.

"Lucija must've totally manipulated you too. So if they were the brains, what are you?"

I want to continue asking questions, but the lights in the hallway turn off. That throws me off my game. It's completely black.

A deep slash forces itself into my lower abdomen, he has stabbed me. Fear creeps back, so I swoosh around the metal bar, only hitting darkness. "Is that all you've got, stabbing me in the dark?" I yell out, more as a way of injecting confidence into myself than anything else. The truth is the anguish has returned with a vengeance, amping up my body in the worst of ways. There are tingles everywhere, and I'm off-balance. I yank my phone out of my pocket and turn the torchlight on.

From left to right, up and down, I light up the entire hallway, but nothing. I purse my lips and breathe out a little deeper than I have been for a while. The killer is gone. Why though? He could've so easily killed me there and then, finishing what he started.

A horrifying scream echoes from the main hall. It's Ingvild. She's in danger. Not her, I can't lose her. My abdomen signals me to be cautious. I've been through worse, Ing first. I sprint towards the end of the hallway, still staying alert for the killer to pop back up. I run past the different rooms, but there's no time to play hide and seek. I need to find Ing. I run down three flights of stairs as fast as I can. I swing open the door that leads to the main hallway, which is thankfully lit up.

All dead. They're all dead.

Chapter 51

INGVILD

Oliwia comes rushing into the main lobby, still holding onto that bar for dear life. She doesn't know where to look first. That's exactly how I felt a second ago.

"All the victims?" She asks me in a shaky voice.

"I-I think so, Liv." Then I spot the wound. "Damn, he got you too? Are you okay?"

"I'll be fine."

Ten corpses have been hung up on the rusty meat hooks. Some of them are still bleeding; others have the most disgusting smell one could imagine. When I first saw them all, I knew Karel was hanging there too, but I couldn't face him yet. So I looked elsewhere, to the other bodies. That couple from the night train, at least I think so, because not much of the girl's upper body remains. Whatever happened to her had to be horrible. Oliwia must've been right about that scream. Something *was* off there, and none of us took her seriously. Then there's Agueda, Mihails, and Andreea. Agueda's face has these massive holes in the side, which make my stomach churn. There are two other people I don't recognise, but I suppose they were killed the same night as Mihails and Andreea, according to what Balazs said about the news. Then that old lady from the chain bridge. Poor woman—no idea how she ended up dead. Perhaps she tried to help Karla out. Then there's Szofi's body, hung headless—a gaping fleshy wound staring down at us—with the meat hook penetrating her chest. And yes, Karel. He's hanging there too. I can't take it. Seeing his dangling feet makes me feel even weaker. I need a hospital soon. Very soon.

Oliwia walks around the display of morbidity, deciphering who's who. When she moves towards Karel's body, she catches my eyes.

"Ing, I'm so sorry, you shouldn't have to see this."

She moves past the other victims and hugs both Balazs and me, and I experience immense relief having her with us again.

"It's like he's showing off his prized possessions." she continues, a tone graver than I'm used to hearing from her. "We're in his world. This entire building is just a maze full of tricks and games."

"A bit like Saw," Balazs adds.

"Exactly. But—" She furrows her brows. "Karla. Where's Karla?"

I hadn't realised it yet either. My mind's been too obsessed with not peering at my dead boyfriend.

"Why is her body not on there? It seems like everyone else is - here."

"Well, she died on that ferry. There were people everywhere. The police must've gotten there before the killer could do anything."

"Possible. But how did the old lady end up here then? I saw her on the bridge."

"Me too. No idea."

Balazs scratches his cheek. "What about Andreea and the

200

rest? They made it into the news, so surely they must've been in the morgue or something. How would a killer be able to get all these bodies here?"

"Connections," Liv replies. "LeBeaux had a lot of connections too, being a detective." She seems to be deep in thought. Something snaps her out of it. "Balazs!" she yells.

"Yes, what?" He appears startled by Oliwia's sudden burst of energy.

"That birth certificate. What did it say?"

Chapter 52

BALAZS

I try to think hard to see what I remember. I'm not sure how I can help though. I want to, it's the only thing keeping me distracted from the horrors that await me after tonight. "Nothing specific. It was just a normal Hungarian certificate. It was a woman's."

"What was her name?"

"Katia Horvat. Quite a typical Hungarian name, not really of our generation though."

"What about the year of birth?" Oliwia wonders.

"I didn't get a chance to see all of that. We only looked for a second before Karel—"

"Stop." Ingvild cuts me short. "We know what you mean."

"So that's it? Nothing else?"

"I'm sorry, I wish I could tell you more. Does that name ring a bell?"

They both think for a moment.

"Not at all," Oliwia admits. They look disappointed. I keep failing people tonight. There's got to be a way to make things right. Even something small. Then an idea pops into my head. "The folders were over there by that desk, right?" I point to the right corner. "Maybe there's still some info there."

We all rush to the desk, keeping an eye out for the killer who could pop out of the shadows, but there are no more files to be found.

"Open the drawers!" Ing speaks out, her voice hoarse and faint at the same time. It worries me to see her like this. We should get her to a doctor as soon as possible. I open the drawers underneath the desk; there are three on the left side. There's nothing in the top one. Nothing in the second one either. I open the third one. A folder.

We exchange nervous looks as I open it.

"Well?" Oliwia asks impatiently.

"They're adoption papers. It's the same name."

"What about the year of birth?"

"Wait, let me check if—here. Here it is. 13 January 1976."

"Seventy-six? That makes her—how old?"

"Forty-seven. Is there anyone you could think of?"

"Hungarian woman of that age? I mean, no."

"She was adopted though," Ing chimes in. "What if her name was changed? What if it's LeBeaux?"

The lights go off in the main lobby. We all scream and grab onto each other. This killer has got some sort of an obsession with lights, for real. Cut it out already. It's mad how powerless you can feel once your sight is stripped away from you. I didn't think I'd still have fear left in me after losing Szofi, but I guess I was wrong.

A slow clapping sound is gliding closer to us.

"Wait, torchlight!" Oliwia hurls as she takes her phone.

"Did you hear that?" Ing queries. "Someone was clapping. Someone's here."

Oliwia lights up parts of the lobby, but we can't see anybody.

"I swear I heard clapping," Ingvild repeats.

"I heard it too," I confess. "The killer is here."

Chapter 53

OLIWIA

I keep turning around, lighting up parts of the room, but we still can't find anyone.

"Peek-a-boo!"

Karel's face hits the light so bright we all scream. The lights go back on.

"You?"

The heartbreak in Ingvild's tear-filled eyes chokes me up.

"I don't want to see tears in your eyes, babe," Karel replies with a blank expression. Terrifying to see him emotionless like this.

He swirls the meat hook in his hands towards Ingvild. The hook swings in the direction of her right eye, slashing deep into her. The blood spouts out violently. I don't understand what I'm seeing. None of us do.

"You're the killer?" Ingvild mutters, blood streaming down her face from her eye socket.

"Yes, hon, me. You can't keep surviving these long chase scenes. It's just not realistic."

She coughs up thick splotches of dark maroon blood, looking helplessly at him and then at me with her left eye.

I run to help her, but her knees have caved, and she falls to the ground.

Not her. Not Ingvild.

Her entire body is shaking. I lower my body and hold her cheeks with my hands. "I'm so sorry, boo. I wish I—"

"I love you, Liv." She manages to get out before her eyelids close. I hurl out the most intense scream I've ever screamed. Not her, she's always been there. "Please, don't leave me, Ing. I can't do this on my own." My heart feels like it's being ripped out of my chest; I won't do this. I can't. Not without the one person who's stood beside me.

The tremors stop, her lifeless body limp in my hands. I need to wake up—there's no way this is actually happening.

"A bit unceremonious, isn't it?" Karel laughs. "She was supposed to die after her long solo scene, but the bitch just wouldn't die. Not as dramatic of a death scene as I had hoped for her, but oh well. Good riddance." He pulls out the meat hook as Ingvild's head jerks involuntarily, spewing out more blood. I jump back and look away.

Balazs is standing next to me, equally shocked. "I—I don't get it," he mumbles.

"Well, you are a bit new to all of this, right? Makes sense. You and sis weren't even supposed to be part of this. You ruined my acronym game. Extremely annoying." Karel talks as if this is the most mundane explanation ever. "My death? Not real. I was hung up by a harness onto that meat hook. And before? Good ole killer kept switching the lights off when we put on some practical effects. It helped that it was behind glass too, so you wouldn't notice it was fake blood. We made sure you didn't have time enough to check up on me. That's where the gas came into play."

I am still reeling from what has happened a moment ago; a

lot of this isn't registering. The ringing in my ears starts.

"We?" I ask.

"Well, obviously it hasn't all been me. This time around I had to stick by all of you to push the next victim in the right direction."

"This time around? Do you mean that—?"

"Oh come on now, Oliwia. Don't play daft. You're the slasher buff, where's your knowledge now? The past always comes back."

"What do you mean?"

He kicks his right shoe into Ingvild's face. More blood. "What do you *mean*? Are you *trying* to make me angry? You said it so many times. LeBeaux and her team."

Balazs is trying to catch up. "So you were part of it since the beginning?"

"See, even newbie here gets it! Points for the Hungarian."

My mind is racing, rushing back and forth from the past to the now. Karel was never stabbed or stalked in the past. He texted us to go to the library. He showed up at the concert hall before Marieke died.

"So who did you—?" I can't finish that sentence.

"Ayat and Marieke. I wish I could say Alzbeta was mine too, but LeBeaux did all of that on her own. Well, the killing bit. I texted Alzy. 'MIOLAA' and all that. I thought it had a nice little '90s campy touch, you know? Texting your victims. It made it all a bit more fun. Well, I guess landlines would've been properly '90s, but who the heck has landlines anymore?"

Ingvild's body spasms for a split second. Balazs and I shriek.

"That's normal. She'd dead though—don't get any ideas."

He's so matter-of-fact about all of this, I can't fully believe it's really Karel.

207

"Right, so I can't give everything away yet, 'cause that would be a bit too easy, but you've both made it this far, so you deserve a bit of an explanation."

Balazs looks at me, I can tell he is trying to come up with a plan, but in all honesty, I am too enthralled in this far-too-easy explanation. Karel is eager to tell, and I'm all ears. He is loving the attention.

"That birth certificate was the first clue. I clapped because my girlfriend, or should I say ex"—his smile is pure evil—"anyway, she figured it out. LeBeaux. She wasn't born with that name."

"Horvat," Balazs whispers.

"Yes, new guy, Horvat. Katia Horvat was her birth name."

He stops his rant and tilts his head at me exactly the way the masked killer did. Guess they've all been studying some Michael Myers' moves. Unoriginal pastiches, they are.

"So?" I ask, as flatly as possible.

"So, you can't put two and two together? She was born here."

"Well, duh," I reply nonchalantly. I can't allow him the pleasure of mansplaining on top of everything.

"Not like Hungary here. *Here.* LeBeaux was born in this building, Liv."

"What?" I can't hide the shock in my voice this time around. "Is that why we were brought here?"

"We're getting somewhere. Go on then, Polish superhero; work that brain of yours."

The numbness in my left arm is becoming more apparent. His voice reverberates in my ears. *Not now, stay here. Ground yourself. Hold onto the metal pole.*

"I don't get it. Who is the killer then?" For the first time, Karel shows some emotion. He looks hurt.

208

"I am," he replies, fully offended.

"I mean besides you, the one who's wearing the mask this entire time in Budapest."

Karel doubts himself for a moment. "I can't give you that big reveal yet. I think I've given you plenty to work with, countess. I mean, it's been tons of work for me. I've been subtly hinting at you coming to Budapest for years now to Ingvild. The two of you thought it was *your* idea, I'm sure, but I'm the one who kept mentioning the Surrealist galleries. Ingvild was more into Surrealism back then. Her little Art Nouveau obsession came later, remember? After a while you become convinced it was your idea all along, right? I had to get you here. To this building."

I hate this. I've never been a fan of riddles, but right now I'd like to knock the answer out of his dumb skull.

"You can't figure it out, can you?" He smirks, the cockiness on that face of his ready to get slapped off.

"Oliwia, does any of this make sense to you?" Balazs pleads, hoping something clicks. But it doesn't. I change strategy, time to wind his little ego up.

"Those lights though. The cheapest possible gimmick. Switching the light off so the killer— I mean the real one, not you— can hide again? Really? Ran out of budget, did you?"

I'd like to think Karel is a bit thrown off by that comment. There's something else I've been ignoring though. The real demon. My PTSD has been silently creeping in, wrapping itself around my chest, strings of ivy tightening up my vessels around my arms. As tough as I try to be in front of Karel, I am at the point where I can barely ignore it anymore. There's an attack coming on. I try to signal Balazs, but he can't know the symptoms. It's an invisible monster.

The sights and sounds blur out, the tunnel takes over and echoes dance around in my head. It's too much to cope with. I can't anymore. I want to be that Final Girl, but I'm not the person I was before all of this happened.

I'm done.

Chapter 54

BALAZS

Something is happening to Oliwia. Her eyes are glaring into nothingness. She looks completely frozen. I've seen this before, in New York Cafe. It's that anxiety thing they all explained. How do I get her out of it when Karel is right there?

He smiles in the most evil of ways. She's powerless.

Chapter 55

OLIWIA

"Livvy girl—"

Gotcha.

"Only Karla gets to call me that!" I reply and smack Karel's face with the metal bar. It bears down heavily on his temple, splotches of blood spraying on my face. Balazs flinches. Karel lets out a childish shriek and stumbles over Ingvild's body, onto the floor. Karel knew all too well what the symptoms of my disorder look like; it was time I used his knowledge over me against him.

"Again, hit him again!" Balazs encourages me. So I do.

This one's for Karla, you bastard.

The pole strikes his face again as Karel howls in agony. He holds up his hands as streaky streams of red run down his face.

"Stop, stop! You need to know the rest of the story. You want to know why this is all about you, right?" He stumbles over his words, barely holding onto any dignity left.

I do want to know. But I've got him right where I want him.

"Kill him!" Balazs practically begs me, standing behind me.

Karel glances at Balazs, then at me. "But the end of the story—" He coughs up some blood. Taste of his own medicine. He is lying there like a helpless little lamb begging for mercy.

"Exactly. This is the end of your story. Say hi to Lucija."

I lift up the pole and move it to a perfect vertical angle. The eyes of fear, defeat. I'm scanning to see if I can find any remorse in there, but there is none. He doesn't deserve second chances.

"Liv, please." He pleads.

Heck no. I pierce his entire face in one swift, pulsating move. His arms and legs stretch out in a jerky fashion, his entire body shocked. His fingers twitch for a second, grappling onto life.

Then it's done. His arms flop down onto the floor, a mere thud signalling the end.

He's dead. No big finale for him, a quick death. He doesn't deserve more than that.

Chapter 56

BALAZS

A smile runs across my face as I see Karel's lifeless body, a puddle of bloodied misery. He might not have killed Szofi, but he was partly responsible. Retribution. Not that it will bring my sister back, but he got what was coming for him. Oliwia pushes her boots onto his chest as she heaves out the pole from his face.

"We still need this," she utters with determination as she turns around and nods at me. "The killer's still out there."

"Do you think this could perhaps be the point where we call the police?"

"No. There are too many connections here. The killer getting bodies from the morgue, LeBeaux being a detective. I think it's an entire network. If we're smart about this, we go rogue."

"A network of what, killers? Like a group?"

"Well, there are at least four. LeBeaux, Lucija, Karel, and whoever is behind that mask. Who knows who else is behind this or who is really calling the shots? I'm not taking any chances with the authorities. This is *our* battle now, Balazs. I'm sorry I got you dragged into this."

As much as I want to convince her she can trust the police,

I do understand her point of view, and perhaps she's right. Pulling off an operation like this can't be easy. Her face shows the pain she's in as she touches her abdomen, there's more blood coming out. She sees that I've noticed. "It's fine, I'm a tough cookie."

"That I've noticed. Why *you* though? Karel insisted this is all about you."

"I'm not sure." She throws a peek at his body and closes her eyes when they hit Ingvild's. "It's something about LeBeaux's adoption file, obviously. Perhaps the killer is related to her."

"What if Karel is?"

She looks back at his face to spot any resemblance to LeBeaux before apparently realising how messed up he looks. "I don't think so, but we can't be sure."

She pauses for a split second. "You." Her entire posture changes.

"What about me?"

"You're Hungarian. What if there's a connection to you? It would make sense. You're from Budapest."

That thought unsettles me. "Not originally. I mean, yes, Hungarian, but I moved to Budapest when I went to uni here."

"Still. What are the odds of us meeting you and you ending up here? With me?"

Something about the way in which she is slowing down as she speaks alarms me.

"What are you insinuating, Oliwia?"

"Out of all the people we could've met on this trip, it ends up being you. A coincidence?"

This sinking feeling in my stomach tells me she is about to turn against me. "Oliwia, I have nothing to do with this. At least as far as I'm aware. Why would I? My sister—"

"The ultimate sacrifice in some messed-up scheme. Step away from me, Balazs."

She shifts the pole, coated in blood and slivers of flesh, towards me.

"You have to believe me, Oliwia. There's still a killer out there."

"And maybe you're another one."

She takes a confident step, inching closer. "I told myself I wouldn't trust anyone again until all of this is finished. That includes you."

A razor-sharp sensation hits my upper arm. Oliwia hurls and points the bar higher. "Behind you!"

I peer over my shoulder and feel the large butcher's knife slicing through my skin, scratching the bones underneath.

"Duck!" I hunch down as Oliwia swirls the bar in the direction of the killer, but she misses by an inch.

The knife is pulled out of my arm and jammed into my shoulder blade. My knee-jerk reaction is to elbow the killer in his stomach. As he hovers around momentarily losing focus, I pull out the knife. The intensity of the pain makes my skin crawl. The sweat beads run down my neck, making me shiver.

Oliwia seems unsure what to do, so I reach out my hand. "Trust me, please." She meekly nods her head and holds on tight as we both jog to the main doors, pushing through the pain. The killer stands up again and walks to us. There's no rush in his stride, no panic.

I bang on the door and try to open it, but the bolts are locked. Of course they are. Oliwia does the same with the other door to no avail. I scan the large lobby, looking for a way out as the figure gets closer and closer.

We're locked in.

Chapter 57

OLIWIA

The killer pulls out another knife and flings it in my direction. I jump to the right, causing the knife to land in the main door.

"Run, now!" I direct my stare at Balazs as we both run past the killer into the back of the main lobby. The figure is struggling with the knife. This is our chance. We're both being slowed down by the knife wounds.

"Now what?" Balazs asks me in despair.

I survey the room, trying to find anything that can serve as a weapon for him, but except for some chairs and a desk, nothing else is lying around. My heart is running a million miles an hour. The figure pulls the knife back out and turns around, his chest filled with rage, the deep ins and outs of his breathing look more menacing than ever. This person is taller and stronger than Karel ever was. This is definitely not Erik either. That dude's scrawny body could fit into the killer's imposing stature at least twice. I want to strike him down the way I did before, but the fatigue and defeat after Ingvild's death make me unsure. This feels endless. This needs to be over with, now.

"Now we get the hell out of here!" I reach out for his hand again. For a small moment, Balazs pulls a faint smile, us holding hands giving some kind of comfort and strength.

"Is there another way out?" he whispers to me.

We both keep our gaze fixated on the killer, who is still standing by the door, calculating his next move.

"There must be. One thing."

"What?"

"Let's not be those dumb slasher people who run upstairs."

"Then what do you suggest?"

"Let's search for a back exit somewhere on this floor. There must be."

We make a run for it. The moment we set off, the killer follows us, this time breaking his calm pacing with a predator's run.

We turn left into a smaller dark hallway, followed by the figure.

"Faster!" Balazs yells. We turn up the dial and pick up speed, flight taking over yet again.

I notice the blood streaming down his neck and arm, but there's no slowing him down.

I find an old fire exit sign at the end of the hallway. "There!" I signal. He sees it as well and nods.

The killer is inching closer, sprinting faster now too. It almost appears as though he is floating through the hallway, the long overcoat serving as gothic wings.

We arrive at the rusty metal door, which is shut as well. I push and pull on the lever with all my might. It is budging a tiny bit.

"Give me your pole!" Balazs yells. I look at the killer, who is seconds away from us, and then back at him. "Now!"

Can I trust him? I need to. I can't do everything on my own. There's no time for hesitation. I hand over the bar.

"I'll hold him back, you crack open the door, I can see it's moving."

"I–I don't know if I can."

"You've got this. You've got more strength than me. I've been stabbed twice."

The killer crashes into Balazs and pushes him to the ground, rolling on top of him.

"Balazs! Fight him!" I shout as I continue pushing into the door. There's a hint of movement. I use my body weight and elbow the lever repeatedly. It hurts like hell.

The killer pulls out his knife and stabs Balazs in the chest. He screams out in frustration.

"Let go of me!" He holds up the bar horizontally at the height of his collar bone, which is serving as some sort of barrier between the two. He is using it more as protection than as a weapon.

I push harder, the metal creaking in its barred-up slots. *Come on, you can't give up now. Balazs needs you.*

"Push him with the bar!" I yell at him, but I can tell he is losing the fight. I keep looking back at the duel whilst breaking into the slots of the door, not wanting to miss a second in case the killer jumps up and throws himself at me or does something horrible to Balazs.

"I don't—I can't." His voice is strained. I've seen this before. Not again. This guy's been there for us the entire time. Why couldn't I trust him? He's lost his own twin sister. What is wrong with me?

The killer stabs him in the chest two more times, the gaping wound becoming darker and larger. Balazs is closing his eyes.

"Balazs! Stay with me!" I stop what I'm doing to go to him, but he stops me in my tracks.

"No! Go—just go. The exit is right there. Go!" He yells. He's crying now, which in turn makes me sob. "Go!"

I propel myself against the door; if I can open it in time, I can save us both. It's opening.

Just a bit more. I've got this.

Another stab. Balazs is thrusting the bar against the killer to push him off, but he knows all too well that it won't work.

The door swings open. I did it. I actually did it. "Balazs! It's—"

I gaze at him, his eyes are closed as the killer plunges his knife deep into his chest one last time.

The figure stands, butcher's knife in hand, and makes his way to me. I rush out the door and close it behind me, using the lever from the outside of the building. I shut it down tightly before the killer can reach me.

It's early morning. The first rays of sunlight hit my sleep-deprived eyes. It takes me a moment to adjust. I breathe in the Hungarian summer air and hear the faint sound of cars passing by in the distance.

I made it outside.

He's locked in, together with the bodies of Balazs, Ingvild, Szofi, and all the others. I lean against the door to stop the killer from breaking out, but nothing happens.

Nothing at all.

He might make his way out from the main door, so I move into the small side street. My mind is still running on all cylinders, ready to be attacked at any given moment, so I keep sprinting down the street.

The faces of my friends and girlfriend are burned deep into my mind. I see Ingvild, Karla, and all the others I've lost in

Brussels. They're all standing in the street, motioning for me to keep moving. My legs are numb, but I need to keep going.

Alone. I've lost everyone. All of them. I'm alone in a foreign country. The anxiety kicks back in, overtaking my whole body. I can't keep running. I let out all the hurt and torture of the past years. A scream I've been too scared to release. I fall onto my knees in the middle of the street and cry.

I've lost everyone.

Every single person.

An old man spots me and talks to me in Hungarian. He bends down and holds my hand. The kindest of gestures. I have no idea what he's saying though.

I shake my head: "Nem Magyar. No Hungarian, sorry."

"Hilfe?" he asks in German.

That I get, thanks to Karla. "Ja, bitte. Help. I need help."

Chapter 58

BALAZS

Szofi hugs me. I knew I'd see her again. We're not the most religious of people, but we both do believe in some sort of afterlife. "There's got to be more than this," she always says. Apparently, there is. She holds my head in both her hands, showing me the widest smile.

"I'm so proud of you for fighting the way you did," she says. "You really did what you could to protect Oliwia. I'm so proud, bro."

I start crying.

"It's all right. Let it all out. It's been a lot, I know." So I do. I allow myself to feel the pain.

"I'll see you around, bro."

That snaps me out of it. "What-what do you mean?"

"I'll be here; don't you worry."

The smell of pure alcohol brings me back. Where am I?

Chapter 59

OLIWIA

The old man, named Arpad—if I understood that correctly—has taken me into his old home. It's as if time has stood still in this tiny apartment. The colours, the dusty furniture—right down to the smell. It's like I've been sucked back into the '70s. I think he lives here on his own. There are photos of him and a sweet old lady, but she's not around anymore, from what I can tell.

He gave me some water, bread, and soup (goulash, I imagine) to regain strength after he sat me down at his cute little plastic kitchen table and took care of my wound. He's asked me multiple times to call the police "Polizei?" but I refused. Not when I've come this far. I want to feel safe, trust me I do, but something doesn't feel over yet. It's *never* over that quickly in slashers. You don't run away from a killer and make it out alive merely by closing a door. Do you? Can it be that simple in real life?

I stand up from the table and walk out to the window. We're on the first floor. I'm not sure what state I'm in now, but the hypervigilance is over. I'm alive somehow. Not really here, but alive. I can't really put into words how it feels after the rush is over and before realisation kicks in. It's not there yet, but I've been in this situation before. I know that ugly phase is ahead of me. That's why I want to savour this moment, soaking in the numbness as long as I can. I look out the window, the factory— or whatever that building really is—in the not too far distance. The showdown.

Screams. For help. I look to the left of the street.

It's him. It's Balazs. He's made it out.

Chapter 60

BALAZS

I guess it's the old school way, putting alcohol onto wounds. It does seem to help a bit for now. I'm lying on this hard sofa, next to a typical old Soviet-style kitchen table.

"So how did this all happen to you?" Arpad asks in Hungarian.

"I don't know where to start. My sister—she died. She was killed." The tears well up again. A part of me had hoped I'd died when I saw Szofi earlier.

Oliwia takes my hand. "Be careful what you tell him. You never know who he's connected with," she whispers.

"This sweet old man? He must be in his eighties. I don't think he could hurt us—ahhh!" I yell out as he puts on more alcohol onto my chest.

All three of us burst out laughing, a release of tension. It's almost too surreal for words. Laughing, as brief as it was, is still there inside me. I didn't know it existed.

"We need to get you to a hospital now," Arpad says firmly. "I'm not too sure what has happened to you kids, but I'm calling an ambulance."

I squeeze Oliwia's hand. "Oliwia, Arpad is going to call an ambulance."

A moment of panic sets deep into her eyes.

"We need to go to the hospital. We both know that."

I believe she's trying to find a way out until rationality sets in. "You're absolutely right. I'm so sorry. For a moment I thought it'd be dangerous there too. But you need it and I guess I do too. I have no idea how you've made it out alive in the first place."

"Szofi."

"What? What about her?"

"She kept me going. I think she was looking over me somehow."

She bites her lip, pushing down the tears. "That's beautiful."

"Ambulance?" Arpad repeats to me.

"Yes, please," I reply politely.

"Balazs, I need to apologise." That catches me off guard.

"What for?"

"For not believing you for a moment. Call it a momentary lapse of judgment. I was so in my own head I didn't believe I could trust anyone. Definitely after Ingvild was— you know." A single tear dances its way across her blushed cheek. "And Karla." A second tear.

"Hey, hey, don't beat yourself up over this. You're human, there have been multiple people you've loved and cared for who have ended up betraying you. Of course you'd be wary of me." I squeeze her hand and try my best to smile without showing her how much pain I'm in.

"Thanks, Balazs. You're a keeper."

"I know, right?"

Chapter 61

OLIWIA

I had no idea ambulances moved that quickly. I can already hear them a couple of streets down. A weight was lifted off my shoulders when Balazs told me he understood why I didn't trust him. He's all I've got left here. The only other person who understands the surrealism of the tale.

"They're on their way over, Balazs, listen." He's still holding my hand, looking paler by the minute. I think he'll make it though. He's got his guardian angel watching over him now.

The doorbell rings. We both sigh. Perhaps safety is finally an option after everything that has transpired today.

Arpad says something to Balazs and steps to his front door. Balazs gives him a thumbs up and pats him on his arm. Arpad shuffles over to the door—the cutest old man tiny steps in his slippers—and unlocks it. I look at the kind man and wait for the aid to come in. Balazs smiles at me through his pain again. He's hiding it, but the master recognises the novice's trick.

It's him.

The killer's here.

The tension spins me back into fight mode.

The figure swings the large machete he was carrying before

down deep into Arpad's head. The poor man hurls his lungs out. The weapon cracks into the middle of his skull, breaking his head in two before the figure lifts the machete again. As the two parts of his head split, I see the killer's mask peering through the gashing wound of stringy flesh. The killer is looking through Arpad's head deep into my eyes. Then, within one grotesque second, Arpad's body sags onto the tiled floor. I scream and run to Balazs, who is only half conscious.

The killer moves quickly and brings down the machete into my upper back. I flop over onto the kitchen table. My face smashes sideways onto the surface. I squeal out the pain.

"Get away from her!" Balazs is back to being conscious, I guess. "Leave her alone!"

He tries to move off of the sofa, but the injuries took a lot out of him. The stab wound in my back stings and reminds me of the library in Europea Halls. My first stab. Lucija. A flash courses through me.

The killer strikes me once again, in the same spot.

I scream.

Black spots speckle my vision. I feel it all at once. The grief, the frustration, the anger, the powerlessness over my own body, the lack of agency.

A third stab.

Maybe the Final Girl doesn't make it out this time.

"No!" Balazs throws the bottle of pure alcohol onto the killer's mask, hitting his eyes.

The figure wobbles backwards and pulls out the machete from my back. I hear some bones cracking and nerves snapping as it happens. These horrific animal-like sounds make it out of my throat well beyond my consciousness as the pain overtakes me.

229

The killer stands back up and penetrates his machete deep into Balazs' stomach. He looks at me with defeated eyes.

"No, Balazs!" I jump up—no idea how I manage to do so— and smash my fists into the killer's broad back. I hit him over and over like a boxing ball, trying to distract him from stabbing Balazs.

The figure turns around and pierces the machete into my stomach. The black spots intensify. I can barely see. Balazs and I both stand there, out of breath and weakened by the stabs and the shock. For a split second there, I had hoped we'd be safe. Panic swirls through my entire system.

The sirens are approaching. They're almost here. A hint of hope.

Hang in there.

The blade slides back into my intestines. I think I hear Balazs howling out my name. I'm not sure anymore.

I see them all, sitting around Grand Place. Alzbeta, Ayat, Marieke, Ingvild, Karla, and me. We're all chatting away, teeming with life. Karla is stroking my back and makes some joke about Marieke's mom factor. The rest of us laugh. The cobblestones are heated up from the evening sun. It feels welcoming. We're all together again.

Now there's just me left. I could join them again. I want to.

Chapter 62

BALAZS

Oliwia's gone into shock again. I can barely stand up, yet I have to try. It can't end like this for us. We've both lost the people closest to us today. I'm not sure which pain is the worst right now. The physical agony or the loss.

Then I see them. Two glistening cleavers on the kitchen counter.

I throw myself at the counter, pick them up and plunge them into the killer's shoulder. There's more power left in me than I thought. The cleavers cut deep into his flesh. He flings back and drops the machete, seemingly confused and hurt. He barely balances himself by holding onto the windowpane.

Finally. He's not invincible after all.

Oliwia's back is spouting with blood. She still doesn't really respond to what's happening around her.

That exact moment, the paramedics burst through the door.

"Oliwia! They're here!" She barely reacts. She lifts her head a bit towards the main door. She's heard me. Bits of intestines peer through her t-shirt, circled by blackened thick blood.

"Stay with us!" I yell at her, and a bit to myself as well.

The team spots the killer and runs in his direction. He's way ahead of them though.

For a moment his eyes cut through mine, then he turns his head and looks outside. He retreats a couple of steps and then jumps right through the window, breaking the glass as if it's just a sliver of plastic, and falls down one floor onto the street.

It's a lot, all at the same time. Oliwia is staring around her, asking where I am.

I run to the shattered window. The killer has already sprinted off into the distance. He barely looks hurt, only a minute hint of a limp. How is that even possible?

There's a bunch of yelling around me. The paramedics team is shouting orders at each other. One of them runs down the stairs in pursuit of the killer. The rest of them whip out bandages and stretchers to bring us to the hospital. I don't take my gaze off the street. I notice the man running after him down the street, but the killer is far gone by now. I want to shout out that he went left, but I know it wouldn't help. The killer would outrun him anyway.

So he's won. Just like that. A melange of relief and defeat engulf me.

I cry out when I'm being pulled onto the stretcher.

"Balazs. Are-are you okay?"

Oliwia is already strapped onto the other stretcher. She still appears out of it.

"I'm here. We've made it."

But he's still out there.

Chapter 63

EPILOGUE: OLIWIA

We knew it wasn't over. Nobody had caught the masked killer. He just disappeared into the morning sun. The entire city of Budapest went on high alert the next couple of days. We couldn't stay away from the cops, as much as I had wanted to. Turns out they'd been looking for us since Karla's death. It came as no surprise whatsoever that they only found us after the killer had escaped.

That one I didn't see coming. Usually in the sequel there's another big killer reveal, but for now I suppose I'll have to settle with Karel. The killer just running away like that means this is far from over. I suppose this was Act Two in the end, not Three.

I exhale and take in the sights of the city around me one last time. My body still hurts a lot, but they released me fairly soon after the operation, so I can go home. Finally. I've been in Intensive Care for over two weeks. At least Balazs and I got a room together, so we had each other to lean on. As much as I want to be alone, having him around has softened the blow, a teeny tiny bit at least. Not for a moment did either of us feel safe though. I've watched Halloween 2 ages ago, Laurie's entire hospital battle was becoming all the more realistic. I was fully expecting an unwanted visit. But nothing. Not a sighting, no news updates, no text messages. That's it for now. Home is awaiting me. Whatever that means without having my group around me anymore.

I wanted to come back here first though. Top of the hill. Where Ingvild and I had our talk. Overlooking the rest of the city. Balazs is holding my hand, the way he has been doing whenever I'm lost in my own world. The glistening lights of the metropolis still manage to impress me. The castle, the bastion, the basilica, the Parliament. They're all there—lit up beautifully— waiting on me to say my final goodbyes.

I intentionally avoid looking at the Chain Bridge. For all the hurt and loss we've suffered here, this is also the city in which Ingvild, Karla, and I found some joy in life again. As brief as that felt, it was there. The strong wind howls and almost throws us off balance. But we're still standing.

My mom whispers from behind us: "Not too long, darling. We have a plane to catch."

Both of my parents are waiting in the limo. Balazs' mom and aunt are there too, giving us some space, but keeping an eye on us just in case someone shows up.

I step towards the limo, pushing away the thoughts of Ayat's final moments, and hug my parents. My dad's crying. He almost never does. Balazs taps my shoulder before I step in.

"Oliwia?"

"It's Liv, remember?"

"Yeah, Liv. Can we please stay in touch? No one else understands me the way you do. You know, except for Szofi. But—" He stumbles over his words, his voice cracking. "You get what I'm trying to say. I don't want to lose you."

"Of course." But I'm not too sure if I mean it, as much as I like him. Any reminder of what has happened is too painful right now. We needed each other in the hospital, but I'm going back to a world full of haunted memories. I need to be on my own right now. Perhaps over time, we can meet up again, however much time that'll be.

He hugs me and gives me a peck on my cheek. By his contorted body posture I can tell his body still hurts too. His tall body wrapped around mine is comforting. There's still safety to be found in some places.

"See you soon, Liv." Both of us well up, but I decide not to extend the moment too much and step into the limousine.

"I'm proud of you, Liv," my dad says, still crying. "So proud."

"We're together again. We won't let anything happen to you *ever* again," my mom promises. That's a strong statement to make. I stare out of the window and give Balazs a final wave.

Ping. A text message. My heart stops.

Unknown Number: *It all goes back to the beginning. It always does. Lovers' lane. All the answers are there. See you very soon.*

About the Author

As someone who grew up in the 90s, Alan Shivers fell in love with the campy, MTV-era type of slashers. He mixes these 90s elements with modern European city vibes in his trilogy Europea Halls.

Next to his love for slashers and all things horror, Alan loves architecture, his Romanian stray dog, meditation and learning different languages.

He is based in Brussels, Belgium.

Subscribe to my newsletter:

✉ https://mailchi.mp/b57ece14816e/europea-halls-trilogy

Also by Alan Shivers

EUROPEA HALLS: A YA Slasher Novel
Welcome to Europea Halls. Only the select few have made it into these prestigious dorms in the capital of the EU, Brussels.

When six best teenage friends get stalked by a serial killer, the campus is on high alert. As the body count piles up, it seems the killer knows a thing or two about slasher movies. Can these girls fight back in time to discover the truth behind the gruesome murders, or will no-one live to tell the tale?

A Ya Slasher Novel inspired by 90s Slasher Movies such as "Scream" , "I Know What You Did Last Summer" and "Urban Legend" with a modern European twist.

Who will the Final Girl be or have the rules changed this time around?

Out on Amazon (eBook and Paperback), free on Kindle Unlimited.

EUROPEA HALLS 3

When the survivors of the summer massacre in Budapest are forced to go to
Brussels, they will learn the hard way that
the final chapter of a Slasher Trilogy always
goes back to the beginning.

OUT 2024.

Printed in Great Britain
by Amazon

37046838R00142